101 GREAT THINGS TO DO BEFORE YOU GROW UP

hinkler

hinkler

Published by Hinkler Books Pty Ltd
45–55 Fairchild Street
Heatherton Victoria 3202 Australia
www.hinklerbooks.com

© Hinkler Books Pty Ltd 2009, 2013

Authors: Sofija Stefanovic, George Ivanoff and Peter Taylor
Editors: Kate Barnes, Kate Cuthbert and Louise Coulthard
Cover design: Ginny Westcott
Internal design: Michael Raz
Internal illustrations: Brijbasi and MPS Limited
Typesetting: MPS Limited
Prepress: Graphic Print Group

ISBN: 978 1 7436 3165 2

Printed and bound in China

Contents

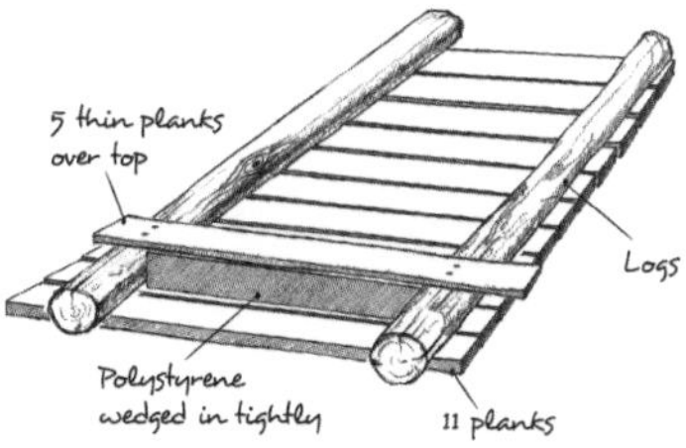

5 thin planks
over top
Logs
Polystyrene
wedged in tightly
11 planks

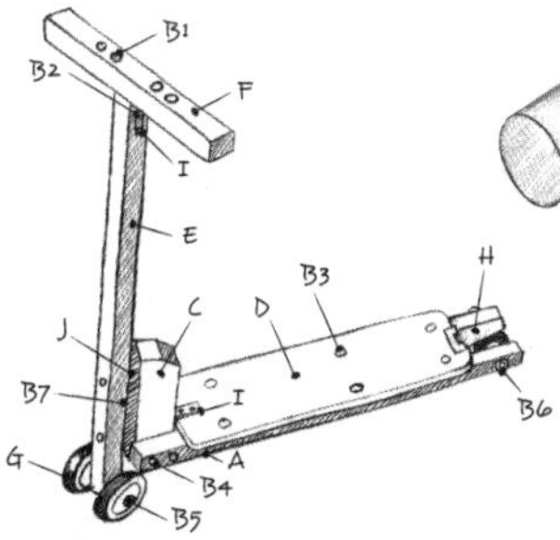

B1
B2
F
I
E
B3
H
C
D
J
B7
I
B6
G
A
B4
B5

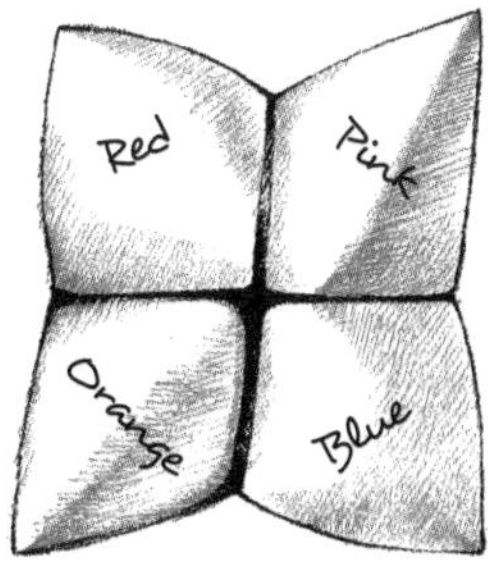

Red
Pink
Orange
Blue

Science

Gadgets

Trickery

Survival

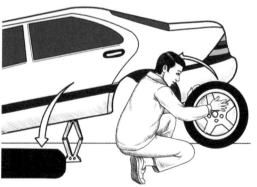

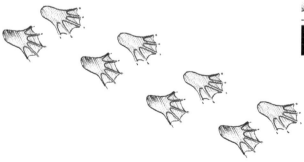

Introduction

Everyone knows that grown-ups are really just big kids. It doesn't matter how young or old a person might be, there's always time to learn and discover new things.

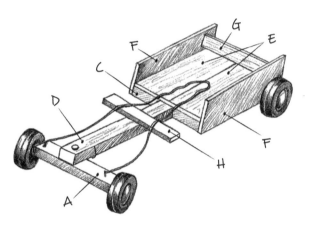

These pages list 101 things to do before you grow up. The ideas presented in this book can add a whole new dimension to living. They can also help you discover new activities and talents – there's never an excuse to be bored. There are a few projects that might be exclusively for the young, but there are plenty of suggestions that grown-ups can explore with children, or even try themselves!

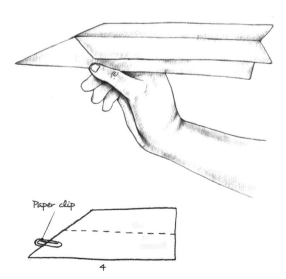

Paper clip

4

Discover the secrets of scientific cause and effect. Experience the simple fun of building a paper airplane that flies further than anyone else's or a kite that flies higher and higher as you run to keep up with the wind.

Plastic with 2-3 cm (1 in) margin around frame

You may have watched kite surfers at the beach on a windy day, flying over the waves, defying the odds, and wished that you were out there with them. Why not? Test your skills to the limit and feel the exhilaration of achievement – after all, this is just an extension of building that first kite.

If you have the urge to write a story, do it! Don't put it off – you might have an epic novel inside you, just waiting to be written. Many illustrious authors didn't start writing until they were well down the track of their life's journey. Just imagine how many more wonderful stories there would be if they'd started sooner!

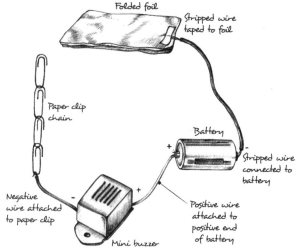

	1	2	3	4	5	6	7	8	9	10
BLOW	C	E	G	C	E	G	C	E	G	C
DRAW	D	G	B	D	F	A	B	D	F	A

Learn to play a musical instrument. It's never too late to begin: the greatest rock stars and musicians all started out learning the basics before they mastered their skills. Don't be daunted by the idea of hard work and practice; the rewards are worth it.

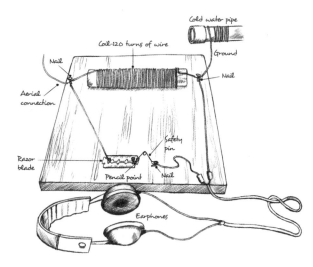

Flick through the pages and find a project that fires your imagination. Create memories, skills, and experiences that will last a lifetime.

Make your very own battery, assemble a burglar alarm from scratch, or create a working radio. There are all sorts of gizmos and gadgets that you can build yourself. Who knows – one day you might use your skills to invent your own amazing machine!

Venture outdoors into nature. Discover how to build a shelter, find water, or start a fire. There may be times when your survival skills will come in handy. They could save a life: it might even be your own.

And remember, even if you have "grown up," you might want to try some of these activities yourself. After all, there's a child inside all of us!

CONSTRUCTION

Make a paper plane

Paper planes come in all shapes and sizes. There are lots of different ways in which to make them. Some are really simple; others are more complex. But they're all fun. Here are some instructions for a very simple plane that flies really well.

What you need

- A rectangular sheet of paper (A4 size works well)
- A small paper clip

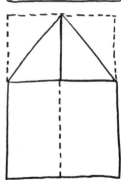

⚒ Did you know?

The art of paper plane making is sometimes called aerogami, after origami (the Japanese art of paper folding).

What you do

1 | Fold a piece of paper in half lengthways and reopen it so you have a crease separating the two halves. The crease will be your guiding line.

2 | At one end of the paper, fold each corner in toward the center, so the inside edges are even with the centerline crease.

3 | Fold the paper in half again, as you did in step 1. Your paper should now have a point at one end – this is the nose of your plane.

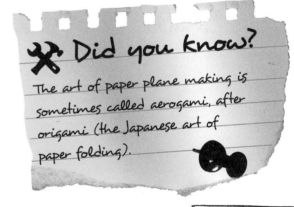

| 4 | Fold each half of the paper in half again lengthways, creating wings. |

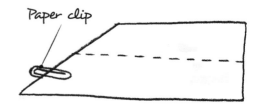

| 5 | Lift the wings slightly so that they are level and attach the paper clip to the front of the plane just below the wings. |

| 6 | Hold the plane just under the paper clip and throw. |

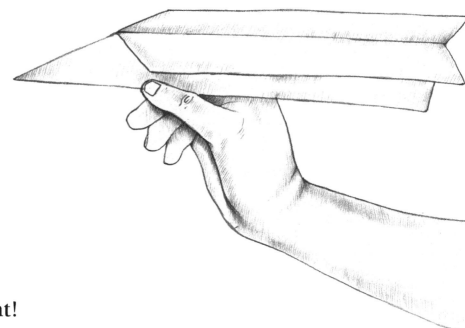

Experiment!

Once you've made a few different types of paper plane, why not experiment a little? Try different sizes and shapes of paper, add different weights onto the nose of the plane, or remove the weight altogether.

During the Second World War, warplanes were often decorated with drawings of everything from shark's teeth to pretty women. So why not give it a try with your paper plane?

Make a kite

Kites have been around for thousands of years. They have been used for entertainment, scientific experiments, and war.

No one knows for sure exactly when they were invented or by whom. But they can be traced back at least 2,800 years to ancient China. Made from bamboo and silk, these kites were used for measuring distances, testing the wind, lifting men, signaling, and communication for military operations.

These days, kites can be used to pull people on surfboards, landboards, and even kite buggies.

People compete in kiting competitions, including stunt kiting.

Over the years, kites have been made from all sorts of materials, including paper, plastic, foil, and fabric for the sail; and wood, plastic, fiberglass and aluminum for the frame. Kites come in all different shapes and sizes, including box kites and arrow-shaped kites. The most recognizable kite shape is the diamond. Here are some instructions so you can make your own diamond-shaped kite from simple materials.

What you need

- Fishing line

- String or twine

- Sticky tape or masking tape

- Glue

- One sheet of strong, flexible plastic (or a sheet of strong paper), about 100 cm × 100 cm (39.37 in) (such as a heavy-duty rubbish bag)

- Two strong, straight sticks of bamboo or wooden dowelling – one 90 cm (35.43 in) and the other 80 cm (31.49 in)

- Party streamers

✖ Did you know?

Kites have been used for more than just fun on a windy day. In June 1752, American Benjamin Franklin flew a kite during a thunderstorm. Attached to the kite was a metal key. When struck by lightning, the key became electrified, proving that lightning was electricity.

What you do

1 | Make a cross with the two sticks, with the shorter stick placed horizontally across the longer stick, about 30 cm (12 in) from the top. Make sure that both sides of the cross piece are equal in width.

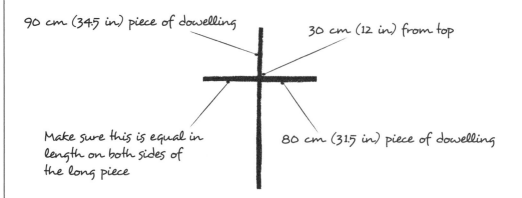

90 cm (34.5 in) piece of dowelling

30 cm (12 in) from top

Make sure this is equal in length on both sides of the long piece

80 cm (31.5 in) piece of dowelling

2 | Tie the two sticks together with the string. To make sure that the joint is strong, put a dab of glue on the joint before tying the string **and** after tying the string. Allow the glue to dry.

3 | Lay the plastic flat and place the stick frame down on top. Using the frame as a guide, cut the plastic into a diamond shape, leaving about 2–3 cm (1 in) for a margin.

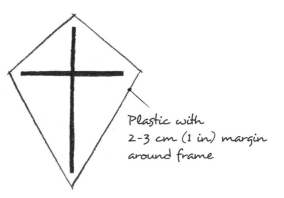

Plastic with 2–3 cm (1 in) margin around frame

4 | Fold the margin of plastic over the stick frame and tape it down so that the plastic is tight.

5 | Tie the fishing line to the center of the frame, where the two sticks join.

Did you know?

Kites have been used during war for signaling, for delivery of munitions, and for observation, by lifting an observer above a battlefield. In modern times, kites have also been used to lift cameras to take aerial photos.

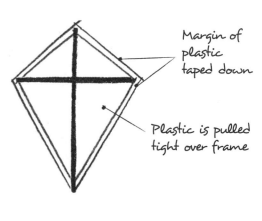

Margin of plastic taped down

Plastic is pulled tight over frame

6 | Attach a few lengths of party streamer to the bottom corner of the kite with tape.

7 | Go outside, wait for a gust of wind, and throw your kite up into the air … and hold on tight to the string!

Decorate!

If you want to decorate your kite, it's easier to paint or draw on the plastic before you actually attach it to the frame.

Did you know?

Kite flying is a professional sport in Thailand.

Build an air cannon

Want to shoot things with gusts of air? It's easy! Just build your very own air cannon.

What you need

- A bucket or large can
- A plastic bag
- A large rubber band

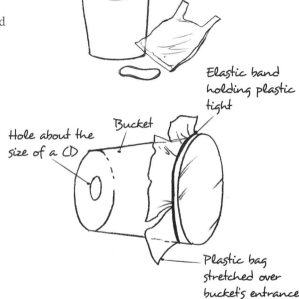

Elastic band holding plastic tight

Hole about the size of a CD

Bucket

Plastic bag stretched over bucket's entrance

What you do

1 | Cut a hole in the bottom of the bucket or can, about the size of a CD.

2 | Cover the top of the bucket or can with the plastic bag. Make sure to stretch the bag tightly, like the top of a drum. Use the rubber band to hold the plastic in place. If one rubber band is not enough to hold it in place securely, add a second or third.

3 | Pound on the stretched plastic and feel the air puff out of the hole.

4 | Aim the cannon at different objects, such as playing cards or dominos, and see if you can knock them over with a gust of air. Try building a house out of playing cards and then blowing it over with the air cannon.

Experiment!

Try putting some talcum powder or glitter into the air cannon before using it. Do this outside, as it can get a bit messy.

Try making an air cannon with a smaller hole. The gust of air will be stronger.

Stronger air cannons can be built using compressed air. These types of air cannons are often used as declogging devices or to fire tennis balls for people practicing tennis.

✖ Did you know?

Compressed air cannons are often used to create special effects for film and television. In Superman: The Movie, to achieve the shot of young Clark Kent kicking a football into orbit, an air cannon was placed underground and the football fired from it.

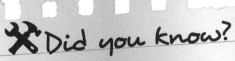

Make a boomerang

Long before the settling of Australia by white people, the indigenous Australian Aboriginals used boomerangs for hunting. The boomerang was a special type of hunting stick that, when thrown correctly, would return to the thrower. It is the effect of air pressure on the two opposing surfaces (the airfoil design), combined with the spinning motion produced by the throw, that causes a boomerang to curve in a circular path and return to its thrower. Making a real boomerang is not easy … but it can be done. It just takes patience and attention to detail.

What you need

- Birch plywood 50.8 cm (20 in) × 40.64 cm (16 in) and 6 mm (0.25 in) thick

- Spray paint or lacquer

- A saw

- Sandpaper with a sanding block

What you do

1 | Photocopy the template in this book, making sure you enlarge it by 50%. Trace the template onto the plywood and use a saw to cut out the shape.

Trace one blade and then flip the pattern on this axis and retrace

2 | Use a sanding block to give each side of the boomerang an airfoil shape. The direction the airfoil faces depends on whether you want a right-handed or left-handed boomerang.

3 | In the middle of the boomerang, blend the two airfoils together. You want the whole surface to be smooth.

4 | Give the boomerang a final sanding with fine sandpaper and then apply a thin coat of spray paint or lacquer to help protect it.

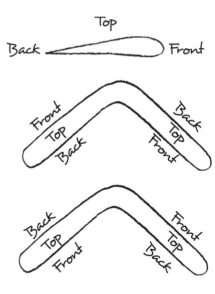

Throwing your boomerang

Don't try throwing it in your backyard. Find a very large, open space – like a park or field. Make sure there is no one else around. You don't want to hit anyone. Remember, the original use for a boomerang was for hunting. A well-thrown boomerang can bring down a fully grown kangaroo.

Hold only the very tip of the boomerang in your throwing hand, with the boomerang's elbow facing forward. Throw the boomerang almost vertical but angled outward slightly. Aim just above the horizon. Throw it hard and overhand, and flick your wrist as you let go.

Once you've thrown it, you can chase after it and pick it up … because it takes a LOT of practice to throw properly. So don't expect it to come back any time soon. But keep trying!

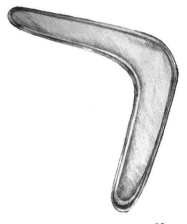

Make a tree swing

Have you ever noticed how kids in movies are always playing on tree swings ... the sort with the old tire on the end? Haven't you always wanted one of those? Well, as long as you have a big enough tree, you can have the tire swing to go along with it. Here's how!

What you need

- A large tree with a thick overhanging branch (You can't do this without a tree ... it's kind of important!)
- A tire – about the size of a tire you would get on a light truck or utility (you could use a car tire, but it may be too small to sit in)
- Nylon rope – about 1.3 cm (0.5 in) thick and long enough to reach the branch, plus 3 m (10 ft)
- Twine
- An eyebolt long enough to go through the branch, with a washer and locknut
- A quick link
- A lighter

What you do

1   Find an appropriate tree. It needs to be a large tree with a sturdy overhanging branch that can safely hold a swing – at least 21 cm (8 in) in diameter. The branch needs to be about 2.7 m (9 ft) high. A hardwood tree, like an oak or ash, would be ideal. Choose a spot along the branch that is far enough away from the trunk to attach a swing, but not so far away that it would cause the branch to bend.

2   You can tie one end of the rope to the branch with a bowline knot, but the friction of the rope against the branch can damage the tree or fray the rope – so this is only a short-term solution. A long-term solution is to drill a hole through the branch and attach an eyebolt with a washer and locknut. Then tie one end of the rope to the quick link with a bowline knot. (Cut off any excess length and use a lighter to melt the end of the rope to prevent fraying.) Then attach the quick link to the eyebolt.

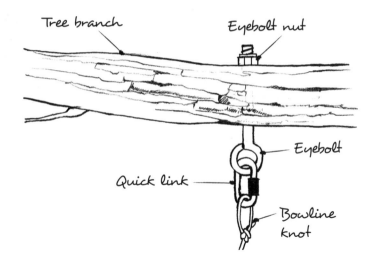

Tree branch

Eyebolt nut

Eyebolt

Quick link

Bowline knot

3   Drill several holes at one end of the tire. This will be the seating end, and the holes will stop rainwater from collecting.

4   Tie the end of the rope to the tire at the appropriate height with a bowline knot. Cut off the excess rope and melt the end of the rope to prevent fraying.

5   Climb onto the tire … and swing!

Make a wormery

Ever wondered what worms do? We all know that worms are good for your garden; that they help keep the soil in good condition. But how do they do it?

A cool way to see worms at work is to make a wormery. Then you'll be able to see how the worms mix up the soil and turn vegetable matter into nutrients.

What you need

- Two-liter plastic drink bottle
- Plastic container
- Black paper
- Gravel (or small pebbles)
- Sand
- Soil (or compost)
- Dead leaves or fruit and vegetable scraps
- Earthworms
- A marker pen

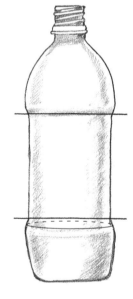

What you do

1   Cut the bottom and top off the plastic bottle, leaving a tall cylinder.

2   Put about 5 cm (2 in) of gravel into the plastic container for drainage.

3   Place the cylinder in the gravel in the plastic container. Put alternate 5 cm (2 in) layers of soil and sand into the cylinder. Make sure that the soil is damp (but not wet). Don't fill up the entire cylinder; leave a little room at the top.

4   Mark the levels of the layers on the cylinder with the marker.

5   Put some dead leaves or fruit and vegetable scraps, broken up into smallish pieces, on top of the layers.

6   Add a few worms (four or five will do).

7   Cover the top of the cylinder with plastic wrap with a few air holes.

8   Put black paper around the cylinder to keep out the light, and leave it for a couple of days.

9   Remove the black paper and observe what has happened. You should see the tunnels the worms have made, and the layers will have shifted and mixed.

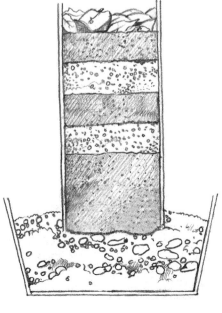

How to hunt for worms

You'll need to find some worms to put into your wormery. How do you find worms?

Turn over stones and dead wood, look under leaf litter, and dig in bare earth. If you still can't find any, thoroughly wet an area of grass, cover it with black plastic, and wait for 30 minutes. The water floods the worms' burrows, and unless they come to the surface, they will drown. This is why so many worms appear on the surface after rain.

Make an ant colony

Ants live in colonies or groups. They tend and take care of their queen ant and her eggs. They usually work together to find food, to fight off any invaders, and to make tunnels to get around. Some ants will bite, and others will sting. Some are quite large, and others are very tiny. Some are black, some are brown, and some are red. There are lots of different types of ants. But they are all really interesting to watch. And the best way to watch them is up close, under glass. So why not make a glass enclosure in which to keep your very own ant colony?

What you need

- Two glass plates – 30 cm × 30 cm (11.8 in) and about 6 mm (0.3 in) thick
- Plasticine or putty
- Masking tape
- A small cardboard box with a lid
- A bendable drinking straw
- A small jar of water
- String
- Saucer of honey
- Soil
- Ants

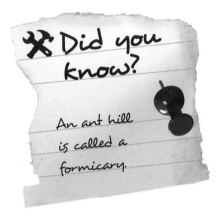

Did you know?

An ant hill is called a formicary.

What you do

1 | Put masking tape around the edges of the glass plates. This will make them safer and easier to handle.

2 | Find a flat, stable surface on which to build your ant colony. Place one sheet of glass onto the surface.

3 | Mold the plasticine or putty into a ring on the sheet of glass. Make it about 8 cm (3.2 in) high, about 2 cm (0.8 in) thick, and 25 cm (9.8 in) diameter. Your ant colony will live in this ring.

4 | Place the jar of water next to the sheet of glass. Put one end of the string into the water and the other end into the ring. This will be the ants' water supply.

5 | Put the cardboard box next to the sheet of glass. Place the saucer of honey into the box. Make a hole in the lid of the box and secure one end of the straw into the hole. Put the other end of the straw into the ring of putty. This is how the ants will get their food.

6 | Fill the putty ring with soil and ants.

7 | Place the second glass plate onto the putty ring. Make sure you keep the colony in the dark except when you are watching them. Ants like it dark. If it is too light for them, they will tunnel toward the center of the enclosure where it is dark and you won't be able to see them!

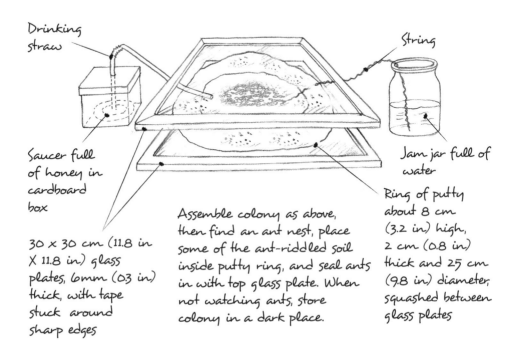

Drinking straw

String

Saucer full of honey in cardboard box

Jam jar full of water

30 x 30 cm (11.8 in X 11.8 in) glass plates, 6mm (0.3 in) thick, with tape stuck around sharp edges

Assemble colony as above, then find an ant nest, place some of the ant-riddled soil inside putty ring, and seal ants in with top glass plate. When not watching ants, store colony in a dark place.

Ring of putty about 8 cm (3.2 in) high, 2 cm (0.8 in) thick and 25 cm (9.8 in) diameter, squashed between glass plates

Collecting ants

It's a good idea to wear gloves when collecting ants to avoid being stung or bitten.

Go outside and look for ants! You often see them walking along in lines. Follow the ants to see where their nest is. With a shovel, dig down into the outer edge of the ant nest. Try to dig down pretty deep so you get the queen ant. She is bigger than the rest of the ants. She will probably be located around a lot of eggs. If you can, dig up some of the eggs, too. Take care – ants will defend their queen and try to bite or sting you. Catching a queen can be difficult … but you need to do it. Your ants will die without her!

Red ants are usually very aggressive – avoid these if you can. Black ants are usually more passive and easier to capture.

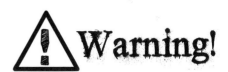**Warning!**

Never mix two ant colonies together; they will fight until death. Collect all your ants from the one colony.

Make a mold garden

Molds are yuck, right? They grow on foods and make them go rotten so you can't eat them. Leave those strawberries in the fridge for too long and they start to go all furry. Yuck!

But molds are also useful! They are a kind of fungus and are related to mushrooms and toadstools. Most fungi live on dead or dying organisms and help recycle the valuable nutrients contained in the organisms back to a form that is usable by other living things. Molds produce chemicals that make things go rotten, which might seem pretty yuck, but if nothing ever rotted, we'd be kilometers deep in garbage!

Molds come in lots of different shapes and colors, and they all have their favorite foods. They reproduce by launching spores into the air that then establish new colonies if they land on a suitable surface.

A great way to see how many incredibly different molds are around on things we use every day is to grow a mold garden. Better yet … grow two of them!

What you need

- Two large plastic containers (takeout containers will do)

- Sticky tape

- Water

- Two labels and a pen

- Bits of different foods – maybe an orange peel, a banana peel, a piece of cheese, a few grapes, a zucchini, a slice of bread or a piece of cake. (Don't use fish or meat though, as they can really stink after just a few days.)

What you do

1 | Dip the bits of food into the water and then put a selection into one of the containers. Put an identical selection of food into the second container so you'll be able to compare the two.

2 | Put the lids on the containers and then tape them down so no one accidentally opens them and eats the contents. YUCK! Put a label on each saying, "Mold Garden. DO NOT OPEN!" This is important, as some people are allergic to mold spores.

3 | Put one container in a fridge and leave the other at room temperature (but not in direct sunlight).

4 | Wait! Nothing much will happen for three or four days. But then you'll see fuzz growing on some of the foods.

5 | Keep watching! Which foods start to rot first? What color are the molds? Is there any difference between the two containers? (There should be, as some molds grow best in heat and some grow best in cold.) Which foods rot fastest? Does any food not rot? They probably all will eventually, but foods that are high in salt, sugar, acid, or preservatives may be much slower to decay.

6 | Keep watching for about two weeks.

7 | When you're finished, throw the containers away without opening them – you may have grown some weird stuff in there!

Did you know?

Substances that prevent the growth of germs (bacteria) are called antibiotics. Today, many antibiotics from different microorganisms are used to treat a variety of infections. The first antibiotic used for medical purposes was penicillin, which is made from a fluffy, blue-green colored mold called penicillium.

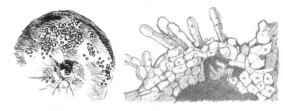

Build a raft

A raft is the simplest form of water vehicle and much simpler to construct than a canoe or boat. There are many different ways to build a raft. You can build a traditional raft entirely out of logs. You can build a wooden raft that uses barrels or PVC pipes to float. You could even build a raft entirely out of soda bottles – it's true! It has been done. You use gaffer tape to stick all the bottles together.

But here are some instructions for building a raft out of wood … with polystyrene to help it float.

What you need

- Two logs 7–8 cm (3 in) thick and 1.5 m (5 ft) long

- Eleven wooden planks, approximately 2.5 cm (1 in) thick, 13 cm (5 in) wide, and 91 cm (3 ft) long

- Five thin planks 5 mm (0.2 in) thick, 13 cm (5 in) wide, and 91 cm (3 ft) long

- Hammer

- Long nails, about 7–8 cm (3 in)

- Short nails

- Polystyrene, about 7–8 cm (3 in) thick

What you do

1   Position the logs parallel to each other, 85 cm (33.5 in) apart.

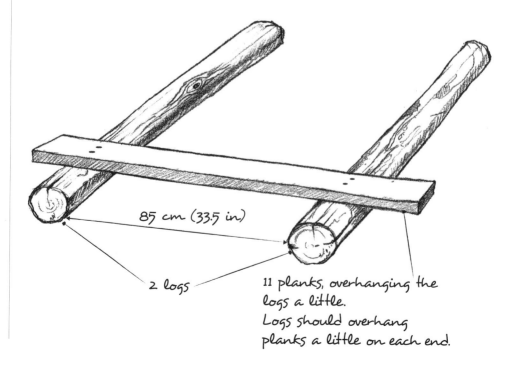

85 cm (33.5 in)

2 logs

11 planks, overhanging the logs a little.
Logs should overhang planks a little on each end.

2   Position the 11 planks across the logs to form the deck. They should overhang each log by a few centimeters. The ends of the logs should extend a little beyond the deck on either side. Nail the planks into place.

3   Turn the raft upside down. Wedge the polystyrene into place between the logs. It's best if you can get one piece of thick polystyrene cut to the correct size – but you can use several smaller pieces, as long as you wedge them in nice and tight.

4   Position the five thin planks across the logs to hold the polystyrene in place. Nail the planks into place.

5   Turn the raft around and place on water. It should stay afloat with one average-sized adult on board.

⚠ Warning!

If you are taking your raft out onto a lake, make sure to wear a life jacket. DO NOT take the raft out onto a river – it is not stable enough and could be dangerous in moving water.

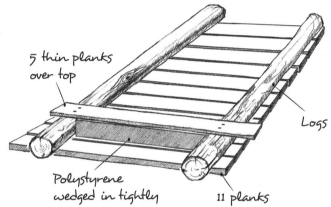

5 thin planks over top

Logs

Polystyrene wedged in tightly

11 planks

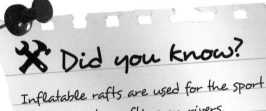

🔨 Did you know?

Inflatable rafts are used for the sport of whitewater rafting on rivers.

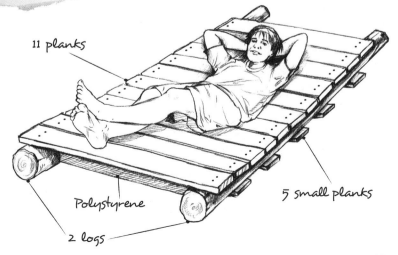

11 planks

Polystyrene

2 logs

5 small planks

Make a wooden whistle

There are all sorts of whistles: little ones, big ones, high pitched, low pitched, wooden ones, metal ones, plastic ones, steam whistles, and musical whistles. Whistles are used by referees in sporting games, by police, by scouts … and by children wanting to annoy their parents with a loud noise!

Want to make your own whistle? Here's how to make one out of wood.

What you need

- Wooden block 7.6 cm × 2 cm × 2 cm (3 in × 0.75 in × 0.75 in)
- An 8 mm (0.3 in) dowel that is 5 cm (2 in) long
- Hand-saw
- Drill with an 8 mm (0.3 in) bit
- Whittling knife
- Sandpaper (medium grain)
- Wood glue

Did you know?

A whistle is classified as a woodwind instrument, which produces sound from a stream of forced air.

What you do

1 | Drill an 8 mm (0.3 in) hole down the center of the block. Make the hole 5.9 cm (2.3 in) deep. Use a lip and spur drill bit (also known as a brad point or dowelling bit) and go slowly to make a clean hole.

2 | Cut the wedge as shown. It is 1 cm (0.4 in) deep and 1.3 cm (0.5 in) long.

3 | Sand one side of the dowel to make it flat. The flat side should be about one quarter to one third of the diameter of the dowel rod. You won't need the whole length of the dowel, but being longer makes it easier to handle.

4 | Slide the dowel rod into the hole in the block. The end of the dowel should be near the spot that the wedge intersects the hole.

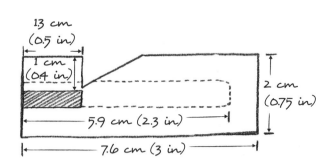

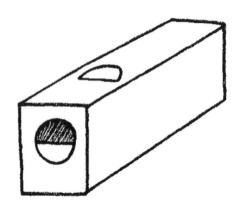

5 Give the whistle a test blow. Get the dowel positioned so it makes the best sound, and then cut off the excess length of dowel (while it is still in the block of wood).

6 Remove the dowel, put a thin coat of wood glue on the rounded part, and return it to the hole.

7 Use a knife to whittle the whistle into a round shape. (Or you could put it into a vise and use a rasp.) (Take care with this step … you don't want to whittle off a finger.) Sand the outside to make it smoother.

8 Start whistling!

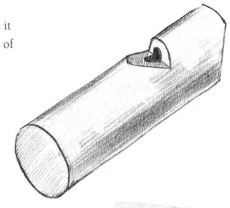

Experiment!

You can make whistles with different pitches by changing the length of the hole. The notch remains the same; only the length of the block of wood and the depth of the hole change. The longer the wood and the hole, the lower the pitch.

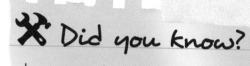

Did you know?

Japanese bird whistles use several small balls and are half filled with water to reproduce the sound of bird song.

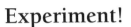

Build a web page

Everyone's on the Web these days. Businesses, music groups, actors … even politicians. They all have their own web pages.

A web page is made up of text and pictures (and possibly sound and other interactive elements), and is built using hypertext markup language (HTML). HTML is a series of tags enclosed in triangular brackets (< >). An opening tag is placed in front of text to format it, and a closing tag is placed after text to stop the formatting.

Once a page is built, it needs to be put on a server (a special computer) so other people can view it. There are lots of ways to build a web page. Here are a few:

Use an automated web site such as MySpace or Facebook. Sites like this use templates and allow

you to make a web page. You can change the look of it: add text, pictures, and music, without ever seeing the HTML tags that make it work. And it is already on a server.

Some word processing and desktop publishing programs, such as MS Word, let you export a document as a web page. Again, you never have to see the HTML tags.

There are lots of programs specifically designed to help you build web pages. Some work like a word processing or desktop publishing program. Others let you edit the HTML tags directly.

Or you can use a simple text-editing program and put in the HTML tags yourself. That is what we are going to do here. We are going to build a simple page from scratch.

What you need

- A computer

- A web browser (such as Internet Explorer, Mozilla, Firefox, Safari)

- A text editor (such a TextEdit, NotePad) or word processing program (such as MS Word)

What you do

1 Open a new document in your text editor.

2 Type in the tags that will create the web page:

    `<HTML>`
    `</HTML>`

These are the tags that tell your web browser that it is looking at a web page.

3 Between these tags, type in the tags that format the body of your page. Your document should look like this:

    `<HTML>`
    `<BODY>`
    `</BODY>`
    `</HTML>`

4 Anything typed between the body tags will actually appear on your web page. Once you have typed in what you want to appear on your page, you can format it by putting the appropriate tags around the text. See the table of simple tags. For example, type:

`<H1>My Web Page</H1>`
`<P>Welcome to my web page. <B>Hope you like it.<B></P>`
`<P>This is my <U>first ever</U> web page.</P>`

It should look like the first screen.

5 When you have finished your page, save the document as plain text. Then change the extension from ".txt" to ".html".

6 Open the page in your web browser. It should look like the second screen.

Simple HTML tags

Body	<BODY> ... </BODY>
Bold	<B> ... </B>
Centre text	<CENTER> ... </CENTER>
Heading 1	<H1> ... </H1>
Heading 2	<H2> ... </H2>
Heading 3	<H3> ... </H3>
Heading 4	<H4> ... </H4>
Italics	<I> ... </I>
Line break / soft return	 ... </BR>
Paragraph	<P> ... </P>
Underline	<U> ... </U>

These are just some very basic HTML tags. There are lots more.

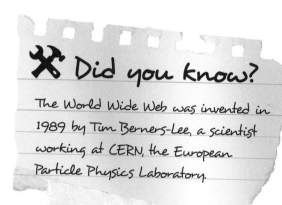

Did you know?

The World Wide Web was invented in 1989 by Tim Berners-Lee, a scientist working at CERN, the European Particle Physics Laboratory.

Build a doll house

Children like to play with doll houses – arranging and rearranging the furniture, settling their dolls in for a tea party, or simply shoving as many toys into it as will fit. Doll houses are also popular with adults. Collectors use them as a place to display their dolls and miniature furniture.

You can buy all sorts of doll houses – from small, relatively cheap, plastic ones from your local toy shop to huge, extravagant, hand-crafted, wooden houses from specialist collector shops. Or you can make your own! Here are some instructions to make a simple doll house from poster board. Once you get the hang of it, you can design your own doll house.

What you need

- Six A4 pieces of poster board 29.5 cm (11.5 in) × 21 cm (8 in)
- A metal ruler
- A craft knife
- A cutting mat
- Sewing pins, 5 mm
- Paint
- Craft glue
- Fabric scraps or wrapping paper

What you do

1. Use one piece of poster board to be the floor of your doll house. Trim about 4 mm (0.2 in) off the length of the board. Cut a piece of fabric to the correct size and glue it to the poster board – this will be the carpet.

2. Set aside another piece of poster board to be the back wall. Cut one or two windows into the poster board – the shape and position are up to you. Either paint the wall or glue some patterned wrapping paper to it to act as wallpaper.

3. Cut two of the poster board pieces as shown in the first diagram. These will be the side walls of the house. Perhaps cut a window into one or both of them. Then paint or wallpaper them.

4. Glue the three walls and floor together as shown in the second diagram. Use the sewing pins to pin the boards together for extra support.

5. Cut down the remaining two poster board pieces to make the roof sections. Each section needs to be 29.5 cm (11.5 in) × 13 cm (8 in).

6. Glue and pin the two roof sections into place as shown in the third diagram: back section first, and then front. Leave to dry.

7. Paint the outside of the house.

8. Move in the dolls and the furniture.

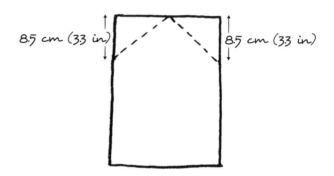

Did you know?

In the 1920s, Sir Edwin Lutyens designed a special doll house for Queen Mary of England. Actually, it was more of a doll palace. It had miniature working lights, running water, a working elevator, paintings, state rooms, servants quarters, and a garage.

8.5 cm (33 in)   8.5 cm (33 in)

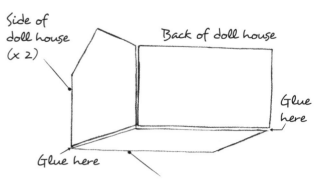

Side of doll house (x 2)

Back of doll house

Glue here

Glue here

Bottom of doll house

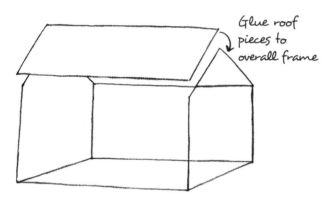

Glue roof pieces to overall frame

Now what?

You can use poster boards to create all sorts of doll houses. You can cut boards to make dividing walls so your house has more than one room. You can use the boards to make several boxes and then connect them all together to make a really big house with lots of rooms.

Construct a billy cart

Do you feel the need – the need for speed? Imagine speeding down an incline in your very own billy cart. Don't imagine it … do it! Build it yourself!

What you need

- Saw
- Carpenter's square
- Marking pencil
- Measuring tape
- Drill and bits
- Hammer
- Wood chisel
- Wrenches
- Dressed-all-round (DAR) timber sizes cut to order:
  - 7.5 cm (3 in)
    two pieces 60 cm (23.5 in) for parts A and B
    (may need adjustment to suit axles/wheels)
    one piece 1.2 m (3.9 feet) for part D
    one piece 38 cm (15 in) for part C
  - 20 cm (7.8 in) × 2.5 cm (1 in)
    four pieces 59.5 cm (23.4 in) for parts E and F

Did you know?

In the USA, billy carts are called soapbox cars because they used to be built from wooden soap crates and rollerskate wheels.

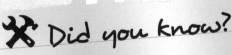

Did you know?

In the United Kingdom, a billy cart car is called a buggy, trolley, cart, or cartie.

- 7.5 cm (3 in) × 2.5 cm (1 in)
  two pieces 38 cm (14.9 in) for parts G and H
  one piece 9 cm (3.5 in) for part J

- Two 60 cm (23.5 in) × 12 mm axles and brackets

- Two 15 cm (5.9 in) wheels to fit front axles

- Two 20 cm (7.8 in) wheels to fit rear axles

- Four split pins to fit axles

- Eight washers to fit axles

- Screws/bolts supplied as kit with axles brackets OR appropriate bolts to fix brackets to parts A and B

- One 11.5 cm (4.5 in) (approx) × 0.95 cm (0.4 in) hexagonal head bolt

- Two 0.95 cm (0.4 in) nuts to fit bolts

- Four 0.95 cm (0.4 in) washers

- Twenty-four 5 cm (1.9 in) × 0.28 cm (0.1 in) flat head nails

- Two 5 cm (1.9 in) × 0.6 cm (0.25 in) cup head bolt

- Two 0.6 cm (0.25 in) washers

- Two 3.8 cm (1.5 in) × 0.315 cm (0.1 in) wood screws

- Two meters (6.6 feet) of rope

Did you know?

In the USA, the first national Soapbox Derby took place in 1934.

What you do

1 | Cut the following from the 7.5 cm (3 in) × 5.5 cm (2.2 in) DAR timber.

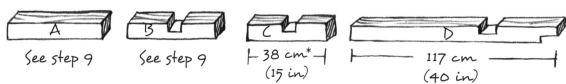

A See step 9
B See step 9
C ⊢ 38 cm* ⊣ (15 in)
D ⊢ 117 cm ⊣ (40 in)

*Note dimension shown for C should equal width of seat made up of two widths of parts E

2 | Cut the following from the 20 cm (7.8 in) × 2.5 cm (1 in) DAR timber.

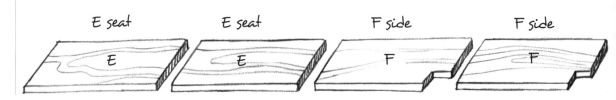

E seat   E seat   F side   F side

E   E   F   F

3 Cut the following from the 7.5 cm (3 in) × 2.5 cm (1 in) DAR timber.

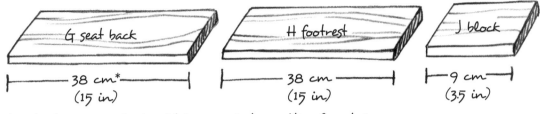

G seat back

38 cm*
(15 in)

H footrest

38 cm
(15 in)

J block

9 cm
(3.5 in)

*Note dimension G should be equal to width of part C.

4 To assemble the frame, bolt pieces B and C to centerboard D, as shown. Use 5 cm (1.9 in) × 0.6 cm (0.2 in) cup head bolts, nuts and washers. The head of the bolt must be on the top side of D. Ensure B and C are at right angles (square) with D. To make a stronger joint, use a standard PVA wood glue.

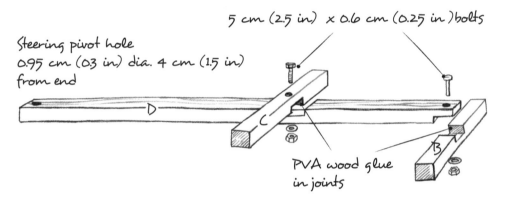

5 cm (2.5 in) x 0.6 cm (0.25 in) bolts

Steering pivot hole
0.95 cm (0.3 in) dia. 4 cm (1.5 in)
from end

PVA wood glue
in joints

5 To fit the wheel brackets, fix the axles brackets to parts A and B using the screws and bolts. The heads of the bolts must be on the top side of part D if used. The front wheel brackets must be positioned to allow rope holes on the forward part of part A and located so the axle position leaves the pivot bolt and nuts accessible for adjustments.

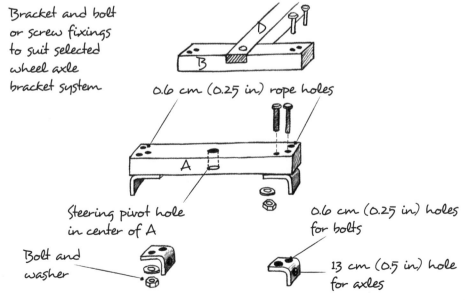

Bracket and bolt
or screw fixings
to suit selected
wheel axle
bracket system

0.6 cm (0.25 in) rope holes

Steering pivot hole
in center of A

Bolt and
washer

0.6 cm (0.25 in) holes
for bolts

13 cm (0.5 in) hole
for axles

6   To assemble the steering, attach part A to D using the 11.5 cm (4.5 in) × 0.95 cm (0.4 in) hexagonal bolt with washers and nuts as shown, with locking nuts on top of part D. (First check that the hexagonal head clears the axle. You may need to sink it into the bottom of part A.)

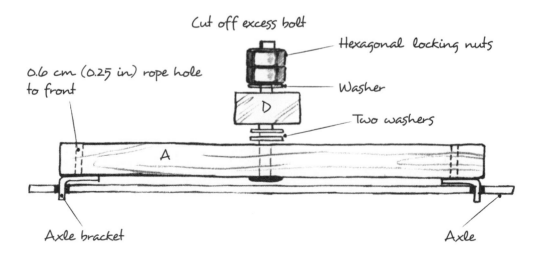

Cut off excess bolt

Hexagonal locking nuts

0.6 cm (0.25 in) rope hole to front

Washer

D

Two washers

A

Axle bracket

Axle

7   Screw part J (the block for the steering lock) to the underside of part D, 3 cm (1.2 in) behind part A, using the two 3.8 cm (1.5 in) × 0.315 cm (0.1 in) wood screws. Thread the rope through the holes in the front edge of part A and tie double knots on the underside of A.

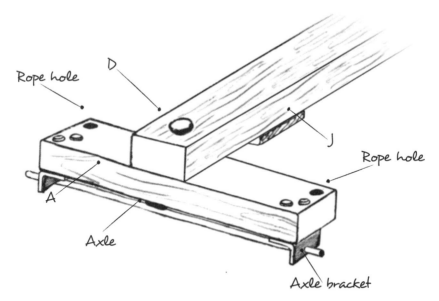

Rope hole

D

J

Rope hole

A

Axle

Axle bracket

8   To fit the seat, nail the seat boards (part E) on the cross braces (parts B and C). Ensure the boards cover the top side of part C and fit flush with the front edge and side (or ends). Use four nails per board, fixing it firmly to parts C and B. Nail the sides (part F) into the edges of the seat boards and into the ends of part C. Note the cutouts on the sides of part F are sized to fit closely over part B. Use four nails per side. Nail the seat back (part G) between the sides of F. The position of the seat back should be adjusted along the length of the side, depending on the size of the drivers. Use two nails on each side of the seat brace, nailing them through the side of part F into the ends of the seat back (part G).

Position of G

F

B   E   C

Footrest H   Seat E

Steering block J   D   C   B   Axle bracket

G fits between sides F

G

F   F

E   E

D

1.9 cm (0.75 in) thick when DAR timber used   Cut out in F fits over B

9   Slide the larger wheels onto the rear axles with the metal bush on the side, or use washers as shown. Insert split pins and bend them open. Repeat this procedure for the front wheels.

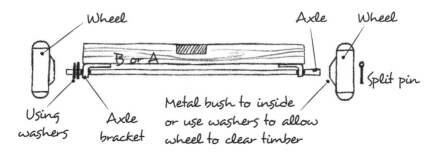

Wheel   Axle   Wheel

B or A

Using washers   Axle bracket   Metal bush to inside or use washers to allow wheel to clear timber   Split pin

10 | To fit the footrest (part H), ensure the wheels are fixed, and then position the driver on the seat to locate the best position. Use two nails to fit part H onto part D.

11 | Round off all corners with a plane or sander and finish the cart all over with your choice of paint.

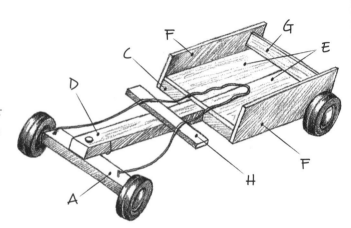

Safety

Wear a dust mask when cutting, planing, or sanding timber.

Be careful when driving your billy cart. Don't go speeding down a steep hill near a busy road. Keep your cart away from traffic and pedestrians.

Construct a scooter

Scooters have been around since the 1920s. Originally they were seen as children's toys, but they have now become a popular form of transport all over the world – from the basic foot-powered variety, through to all sorts of motorized scooters. Just like the children in the 1920s, you can build a basic push scooter out of wood. Here's how.

What you need

- Work stool or sawhorse
- Set square
- Electric drill with a 0.6 cm (0.25 in) drill bit and a 13 mm (0.5 in) drill bit
- Two adjustable wrenches
- Measuring tape
- Square point screwdriver
- Pencil
- Sharp handsaw
- Hammer
- Treated pine wood for runner boards, handlebar and handlebar uprights, 3.8 cm × 5.1 cm (1.5 in × 2 in)

✖ Did you know?

The Vespa scooter, a motorized scooter, started a craze when it was first made in Italy in 1946. "Vespa" means "wasp" in Italian.

- Treated pine wood for the neck, 5.1 cm × 7.6 cm (2 in × 3 in)
- Plywood for the platform deck, 1.9 cm (0.75 in)
- Four eyebolts: two 0.6 cm (0.25 in) eyebolts 5.1 cm (2 in) long with 1.6 cm (0.625 in) hole and two 0.6 cm (0.25 in) eyebolts 7.6 cm (3 in) long with 1.6 cm (0.625 in) hole [J]
- Four 0.6 cm (0.25 in) carriage/coach bolts 4.4 cm (1.75 in) long with one washer and one nut for each bolt [B1]
- Two 0.6 cm (0.25 in) hexagonal head bolts 4.4 cm (1.75 in) long with one nut for each bolt [B2]
- Six 0.6 cm (0.25 in) carriage/coach bolts 7 cm (2.75 in) long with one washer and one nut for each bolt [B3]
- Two 1.3 cm (0.5 in) carriage/coach bolts 12.7 cm (5 in) long with one washer and one nut for each bolt [B4]
- One 1.3 cm (0.5 in) hexagonal head bolt 15.2 cm (6 in) long with two nuts (to lock against each other) and four washers. This bolt is for the front axle [B5]
- One 1.3 cm (0.5 in) hexagonal head bolt 15.2 cm (6 in) long with two nuts (to lock against each other) and four washers. This bolt is for the rear axle [B6]
- One 1.3 cm (0.5 in) carriage/coach bolt 20.3 cm (8 in) long with two nuts (to lock against each other). This bolt goes through the eyes of the eyebolts and acts as a steering pin [B7]

What you do

1   Measure, cut, drill, and lay out
   a. Cut all the pieces of wood to the lengths as shown.
   b. Carefully measure and mark the center of where all the holes are to be drilled.
   c. Next, drill the holes. Note that there are two different hole sizes. The holes for the axle bolts and for the bolts that fasten the runners [A] to the neck [C] are 1.3 cm (0.5 in) holes. All the other holes are 0.6 cm (0.25 in) diameter.
   d. Lay all the pieces out on the floor.

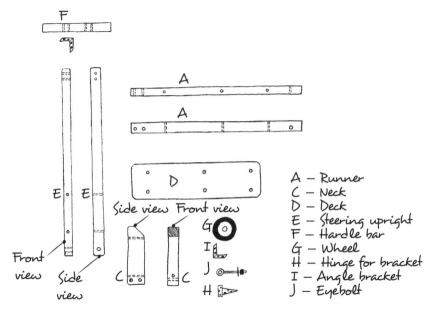

A — Runner
C — Neck
D — Deck
E — Steering upright
F — Handle bar
G — Wheel
H — Hinge for bracket
I — Angle bracket
J — Eyebolt

2   Assemble the handlebar
    a. Bolt the two angle brackets [I] to the top of the steering upright [E].
    b. Then bolt the handlebar [F] in place.

3   Assemble the front wheels
    a. Assemble the front wheels using a 1.3 cm (0.5 in) bolt as the axle.
    b. Place a washer on each side of each wheel.
    c. Making sure that the axle assembly is loose enough to allow the wheels to turn freely, use two nuts tightened against each other to form "lock nuts." This will ensure that the axle assembly does not vibrate loose with constant movement.
    d. Place two eyebolts in the appropriate holes in the steering upright [E].

4   Assemble the platform frame
    a. Bolt the two runners [A] to the neck [C].
    b. Place the remaining two eyebolts in the appropriate holes in the neck [C].

5   Add the deck
    a. Fasten the deck [D] to the two runners [A] with six carriage/coach bolts.

6   Attach the steering assembly
    a. Line up the eye of the eyebolts in the neck [C], with the eye of the eyebolts in the steering upright [E].
    b. Thread a 1.3 cm (0.5 in) carriage/coach bolt through the eyes of the eyebolts to act as a steering pin.
    c. Make sure that the steering assembly can turn freely and then tighten two nuts together at the end of the carriage/coach bolt to form "lock nuts." This will ensure that the steering pin does not fall out or vibrate loose with constant movement.

7   Secure the neck
    a. Fasten an angle bracket to the neck [C] and the deck [D] with screws. This is purely to increase strength.

8   Assemble the rear wheel
    a. Assemble the rear wheel in the same way as for the front wheels in step 3.
    b. Make sure that there is a washer each side of the wheel and also that the wheel can rotate freely, before applying "lock nuts" at the end of the bolt.

9   Add the brakes
    a. Screw a T-hinge to the rear of the deck [D].

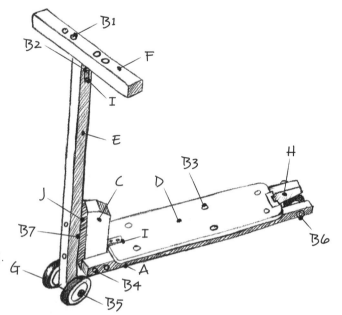

Safety

Smooth, paved surfaces are best; avoid bumpy, uneven, wet, or rocky surfaces. Stay away from traffic!

ENTERTAINMENT

Tell your fortune

A paper fortune teller or "cootie catcher" is a fortune-telling device that possibly dates back to 1600s Japan, where origami was invented. Although they were probably originally invented to hold salt, these little devices are now more commonly used by "in love" people to make "startling" relationship predictions.

What you need

- A piece of paper
- Colored markers
- Pencils

🎸 Did you know?

Believe it or not, it has never been proved that paper fortune tellers work in telling people's fortunes!

What you do

1	Get a piece of square paper. If you only have A4 size, fold one corner over to the opposite side and chop off the bottom.

2	Now, fold the paper in half, then open it up and fold it in half the other way.

3	Fold the four corners into the middle and leave them folded.

4	Turn the paper over and fold all the corners into the middle again.

5	Fold the paper in half.

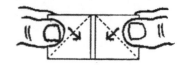

6	Put your fingers and thumbs into the slits made by the corners. Your fortune teller is almost complete.

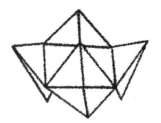

7	Lay it out flat and color in different colors the four outside squares into which you put your fingers and thumbs.

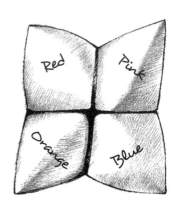

8	Now turn the fortune teller over and write the numbers one to eight on the triangles.

9	Finally, open up the flaps under the numbers and write the words "Yes," "No," "Maybe," "Definitely not," and so on under each half triangle.

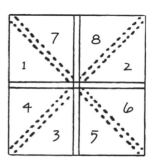

How to use it

You are the teller of fortunes. Your friend asks a question that can be answered with a "Yes" or "No," such as: "Does Victor love me?" You ask them to choose a color. Then you open and close the fortune teller, depending on the number of letters in that color (example: "red" has three letters, so you open the fortune teller three times). Then your friend chooses a number from the ones available on the open fortune teller. You open and close the fortune teller that number of times. Finally, your friend picks a number and you open the flap, revealing the answer, such as: "Absolutely."

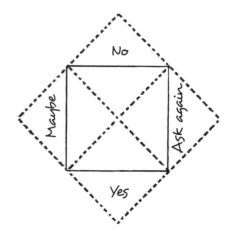

Variation

Instead of writing answers in the teller, you can simply write comments ("You will be famous," "You will fall in love with someone really ugly," etc) and simply "tell" people's fortunes rather than answering a question.

Make a flick book

The aim of a flick book is to create a moving picture. You do this by drawing an image, which moves ever so slightly from one page to the next. So, when you flip the pages, the drawings flow into each other and give the appearance of movement. If you are lazy, you can make a really basic scene, such as a stick figure throwing a ball up and down. If you are an animation genius, you may like to use a couple of phone books to create your epic fantasy battle of trolls and unicorns. For most people, starting with a simple drawing works best.

What you need

- A writing implement

- A notebook (If you don't have a notebook, use a bunch of papers stapled together, or a book that you can deface.)

- A scrap piece of paper

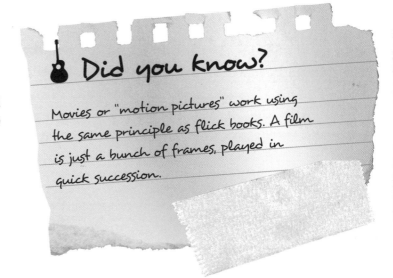

🎸 Did you know?

Movies or "motion pictures" work using the same principle as flick books. A film is just a bunch of frames, played in quick succession.

What you do

1 | You need to make a scene, which changes frame by frame from your first drawing to your last. You start your flick book by drawing your very first frame.

2 | On a scrap piece of paper, draw a rough outline of your final frame – where you want the scene to end. You can use this as a guide when drawing the in-between frames.

3 | The rest is pretty straightforward. Keep drawing, changing your animation slightly as you go from frame to frame. Be patient, as too much change from one frame to another will not give a smooth appearance of movement.

4 | The more patient you are, the better your flick books will be.

Frame 1   Frame 5   Frame 10   Frame 15

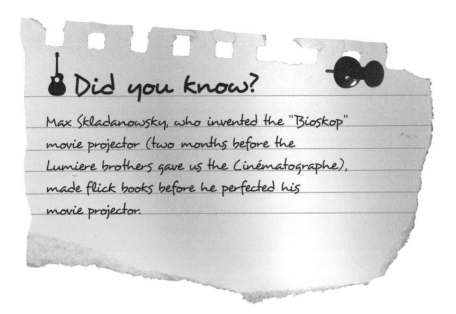

Did you know?

Max Skladanowsky, who invented the "Bioskop"
movie projector (two months before the
Lumiere brothers gave us the Cinématographe),
made flick books before he perfected his
movie projector.

Read a palm

Palm reading, also called chiromancy or palmistry, started in ancient India. In palm reading, the hand is divided into three sections. The fingers and hand shape represent the mind and higher self, the middle of the palm shows the conscious mind, and the lower half shows health and the subconscious. To read someone's palm, you should look at the whole hand.

What you need

• A willing participant's hand

What you do

You can read the palm in any order you like, but here is a sample reading:

1 | Look at the hands. The four hand shapes can be divided into the four elements as follows:

    a. Earth: short fingers and a square palm. This shows honesty and a practical attitude.

    b. Fire: a long palm and short fingers. This suggests a "fiery" and energetic personality.

    c. Water: a long palm and long fingers. This indicates that the person is sensitive and emotional.

    d. Air: square palm with long fingers. This shows creativity and good problem-solving skills.

2 | Look at the fingers. They can be interpreted as follows:

    a. A long pointy thumb represents creativity and a strong personality.

    b. A long index finger suggests good fortune and characteristics of a natural leader.

    c. A long ring finger shows intelligence and imagination.

    d. A long, straight little finger suggests a happy love life.

3 | Look at the mounts of the hands. The fatter or more developed these bits are, the more developed these traits are in a person.

    a. Mount of Venus: sensitivity and compassion.

    b. Mount of Upper Mars: courage and fighting spirit.

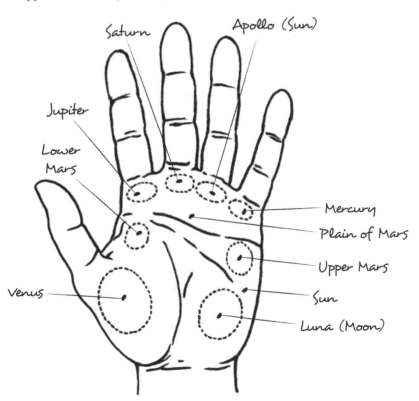

c. Mount of Jupiter: ambition, leadership, and honor.

d. Lower Mars (below Mount of Jupiter): aggression and hostility.

e. Mount of Saturn: wisdom, sensitivity, and introversion.

f. Mount of Apollo: confidence, creativity, and extroversion.

g. Mount of Mercury: good communication skills and a quick wit.

h. Mount of Luna: generosity, kindness, and imagination.

i. Plane of Mars (the center of the palm): If it is dipped, it suggests calmness. If it is raised, It implies a quick temper.

4   Finally, you need to look at the lines of the hands.

a. Heart line: It represents matters of the heart. The cuts and breaks of this line tell us about a person's relationships and love life.

b. Head line: It represents a person's mind. A straight line shows levelheadedness; a curved line shows a person with a more dreamy temperament. A weak line shows lack of concentration.

c. Life line: It represents major life events and health. A long unbroken line shows health and longevity; a broken line can represent illness or a life-changing event.

d. Fate line: It represents prosperity and career success. A smooth long line shows a successful career or a businesslike personality.

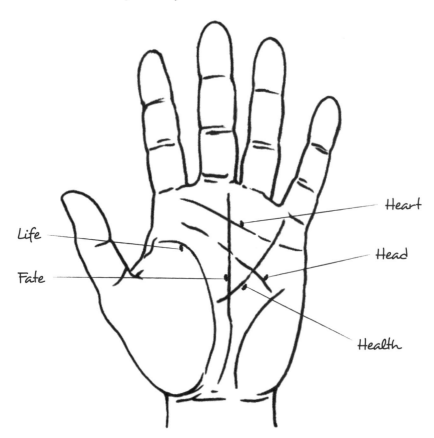

Perform a cartwheel

The important thing about cartwheels is to keep your momentum – once you start the cartwheel, don't slow down. When you get the hang of it, your cartwheel will improve with practice. Before you start your cartwheel, take a look around the space for anything you might break or crash into. Walk around the space with your hands in the air to make sure that there aren't any low-hanging objects you might hit with your legs while you perform the cartwheel.

What you do

1   Stand with your body in an X position, your arms raised above your head.

2   Point one foot in the direction you are going to perform your cartwheel. Choose whichever side feels comfortable. Keep the rest of your body facing forward. Turn your head in the direction of your pointed foot. Your body will follow a straight line, in the direction of the pointed foot.

3   Read the following steps carefully so that you know what to do, but when you are actually performing your cartwheel, you will need to do them in quick succession, so remember the body alignment and positioning.

4   Lift your pointed foot and take a step in the direction you intend to travel to build momentum.

5   Begin to reach down with the hand on the side of your pointed foot (if you have your left foot pointed, then you are going to follow with your left hand). While your hand is coming toward the floor, your back foot will naturally lift up.

6   The hand touches the floor, with your fingers pointing in the opposite direction to where you are facing. Your other hand follows and, at the same time, your pointed foot springs off the ground.

7   Balancing your body on just your hands, keep your back straight. As you perform the cartwheel, your body should again be in an X position, with straight legs. Bring the legs over your head.

8   Land with your opposite toe pointing forward and your hands in the air.

9   The most common sort of cartwheel is a front-to-back. That's when you start facing one way and, after you've done the wheel, you are facing the other way.

10 Some people have a natural talent for acrobatics. If this is not you, here are some basic steps. Practice on a mat or carpet to avoid painful landings.

Walk on your hands

Walking on your hands requires good balance and body strength. It also involves being able to do a handstand, so if you aren't quite comfortable upside down, your ambling adventure will be cut short by a crashing fall.

What you do

1   Get a friend to help by standing in front of you and catching your ankles when the need arises, as this maneuver involves quite a bit of falling over.

2   Put one foot in front of the other and raise your arms.

3   Swing your arms toward the ground and lean over while lifting your leading leg (the one you feel most comfortable using).

4   Bring your hands to the ground as you kick off with the remaining leg.

5   Put your legs up and balance. Once you feel balanced, start taking little steps with your hands. Lean your body slightly in the direction you wish to go. If you think you are going to fall, don't give in to the feeling. Concentrate and keep going.

Scuttle with the crabwalk

The crabwalk is a bizarre-looking trick that involves flexibility rather than balance. There is always one freakish person who is able to bend their legs this far, and if they have any sense of humor, everyone around them will no doubt be familiar with the crabwalk. This is a good way to impress strangers a great conversation starter at parties.

What you do

1. Do a bit of stretching before you start.

2. Sit cross-legged.

3. It doesn't stop there. Use your powers of contortion to stick your arms through the insides of your thighs, so that rather than being on the outside of your legs, your arms are on the inside.

4. Now it's time to use your strength to lift your body using your hands and arms.

5. All you need to do next is take a couple of little steps with your hands and you will be as close as a human being has ever come to looking like a crab.

Juggle

If you want to be an entertaining juggler, you need to be good at it. The key is to practice for ages on your own before you start performing for others.

What you need

- Three objects to juggle, such as small balls or beanbags. Make sure they're about the same size and easy to handle.

What you do

1 | Stand with your feet apart and take one of the balls. You need to throw the balls using your wrists, not your elbows or shoulders. Your forearms should be parallel to the floor.

2 | Get one of the balls. Toss it in an arc (reaching about the top of your head) from one hand to the other. Remember to use your wrists only.

The better your throws are, the easier it will be to catch the ball. Ideally, the ball should land in your hand without you having to move to catch it.

3 | Keep going back and forth until you feel comfortable and you have consistency. The ball should be at the same height and your wrists should be moving easily.

Becoming consistent in your throws is really hard, so take your time and toss slowly until you feel comfortable.

4 | When you have mastered this, get the second ball. As one ball reaches the top of its arc, throw the other ball up and under the first ball. The trick is to master catching the balls and remember to throw consistently!

5 | Finally, introduce the third ball. Hold it in the same hand as your starting ball.

Now, do exactly as you have done so far. Toss the first ball, and when it reaches its arc, toss the second ball up and under. Now, as the second ball reaches its arc, toss the third ball up and under.

As the third ball reaches its arc, toss the first ball again, up and under.

6 | The more you practice, the better you'll get.

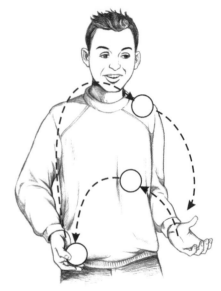

Play the harmonica

Harmonicas are inexpensive and easy to carry around. If you know a couple of tunes, you can entertain yourself and others almost anywhere. It doesn't take long to get the hang of it, and then you just need to hone your technique.

What you need

- A harmonica

What you do

1   Hold the harmonica in your left hand between your thumb and forefinger; it's pretty much like holding a sandwich. The low notes are to the left. Your right hand is free so that you can make all sorts of cupping and wah-wah effects.

2   Look at the instrument. There are two sets of metal reeds in a harmonica. The top reeds respond when you blow. The bottom reeds respond when you suck air through them.

The notes are laid out like this:

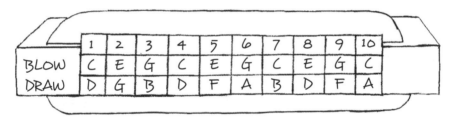

	1	2	3	4	5	6	7	8	9	10
BLOW	C	E	G	C	E	G	C	E	G	C
DRAW	D	G	B	D	F	A	B	D	F	A

3   Familiarize yourself with the music. If you are told to draw 2, it means to suck, or draw on hole 2. If you are told to blow 6, it means blow on hole 6.

The standard notation for harp riffs and tunes goes as follows:

- The number indicates which hole to play.

- The up arrow means blow.

- The down arrow means draw.

So a C major scale is played as follows:

C	D	E	F	G	A	B	C
4	4	5	5	6	6	7	7
↑	↓	↑	↓	↑	↓	↓	↑
BLOW	DRAW	BLOW	DRAW	BLOW	DRAW	DRAW	BLOW

4 | Before you start playing, you need to learn to "pucker up." This means getting your mouth in the correct position. The object is to get a clear, sharp tone from each single note of the harmonica. This is the most important step in learning blues harp.

Your breathing should be natural and not forced. Your lips should be puckered so that only one note emerges clearly.

5 | Practice drawing on each hole, starting from hole 1 on the left. Make your mouth small enough to draw just that one note. Play the note over until you get it right. Move on to the other holes.

6 | If you put your two index fingers over the notes, leaving just one note exposed, you will see how small you need to pucker your mouth to play.

7 | Practice drawing on each hole until you get a clean pure sound.

8 | Now try blowing on each note. To stop and start the note, say the word "ta" as you are blowing. The tip of your tongue will touch the ridge behind your top teeth, stopping the air flowing into or through the harp.

Play!

Here are a couple of tunes to get you practicing, played in C.

Did you know?

Some notes have to be played by bending the airstream over the reed. Bending produces that crying, wailing sound you hear on recordings.

Silent Night

6	6	6	5	6	6	6	5	
↑	↓	↑	↑	↑	↓	↑	↑	
BLOW	DRAW	BLOW	BLOW	BLOW	DRAW	BLOW	BLOW	

8	8	7	7	7	6
↓	↓	↓	↑	↑	↑
DRAW	DRAW	DRAW	BLOW	BLOW	DRAW

6	6	7	7	6	6	6	6	5
↓	↓	↑	↓	↓	↑	↓	↑	↑
DRAW	DRAW	BLOW	DRAW	DRAW	BLOW	DRAW	BLOW	BLOW

6	6	7	7	6	6	6	6	5
↓	↓	↑	↓	↓	↑	↓	↑	↑
DRAW	DRAW	BLOW	DRAW	DRAW	BLOW	DRAW	BLOW	BLOW

8	8	9	8	7	7	8
↓	↓	↑	↓	↓	↑	↑
DRAW	DRAW	BLOW	DRAW	DRAW	BLOW	BLOW

7	6	5	6	5	4	4
↑	↑	↑	↑	↓	↓	↑
BLOW	BLOW	BLOW	BLOW	DRAW	DRAW	BLOW

6	6	7	8	8	7	7	6	9	9	9	8	9	9	7	7	7	7	7	8
↑	↑	↑	↓	↑	↑	↓	↓	↓	↓	↓	↑	↓	↑	↑	↑	↑	↓	↑	↓
BLOW	BLOW	BLOW	DRAW	BLOW	BLOW	DRAW	DRAW	DRAW	DRAW	DRAW	BLOW	DRAW	BLOW	BLOW	BLOW	BLOW	DRAW	BLOW	DRAW

6	6	7	8	8	7	7	6	9	9	9	9	9	8	8	7	7	7	8	7
↑	↑	↑	↓	↑	↑	↓	↓	↓	↓	↓	↓	↑	↓	↑	↓	↑	↓	↓	↑
BLOW	BLOW	BLOW	DRAW	BLOW	BLOW	DRAW	DRAW	DRAW	DRAW	DRAW	DRAW	BLOW	DRAW	BLOW	DRAW	BLOW	DRAW	BLOW	DRAW	BLOW

9	9	8	8	8	6	6	7	7	7	7	7	7	8	6	6	7	8	8
↑	↓	↑	↓	↑	↑	↑	↑	↑	↑	↑	↓	↑	↓	↑	↑	↑	↓	↑
BLOW	DRAW	BLOW	DRAW	BLOW	BLOW	BLOW	BLOW	BLOW	BLOW	BLOW	DRAW	BLOW	DRAW	BLOW	BLOW	BLOW	DRAW	BLOW

7	7	6	9	9	9	9	9	8	8	7	7	7	8	7
↑	↓	↓	↓	↓	↓	↓	↓	↑	↓	↑	↓	↓	↑	↑
BLOW	DRAW	DRAW	DRAW	DRAW	DRAW	DRAW	DRAW	BLOW	DRAW	BLOW	DRAW	BLOW	DRAW	BLOW

Learn to play poker

There are many different sorts of poker. The one we have included here is a solid one to start with – five-card draw poker. After you are familiar with this game, other variations such as Texas Hold'em will come easily.

What you need

- A 52-card pack
- Four or more players

What you do

1 | Gather four or more players.

2 | The dealer is chosen. Dealing to the left, each player is dealt five cards, one at a time.

3 | Each player puts a chip (or money, or matchstick, or jelly bean, or whatever the stakes are) into the pool. Betting starts to the dealer's left and goes clockwise.

4 | Once the cards have been dealt and players have looked at their cards, they can call, raise, or fold.

- If you fold, you abandon your hand, losing the chips you have already bet.

- If you call, you have to put enough chips to match, but not exceed, what any other player has bet.

- If you raise, you must add more chips to what any other player has bet in the round. You must say how much you are raising by and place your chips in the pool.

5 | After this round of betting and folding, the remaining players are allowed to discard three cards or less. They receive replacement cards from the dealer.

6 | This is followed by another betting round. Players can again call, raise, or fold. At the end of the betting, all players must have put the same number of chips into the pool. If you don't do this, you have to fold.

7 | The hands of the remaining players are shown and the highest hand wins the pot.

- The aim of the game is to have the highest ranking hand at the end of the game.

- Aces are of the highest value but can be used as a 1 (values go: A, 2, 3, 4, 5, 6, 7, 8, 9, 10, J, Q, K, A).

- The suits are of equal value.

Tip

Watch the other players and pay attention to their bets. You can tell a lot from the way a player behaves. If a player discards only one card, they either have a great hand or they're bluffing.

Tip

Be careful with your bluffs. If you have a low hand, you may want to stay in the game and not fold, hoping that other players will be intimidated into folding, leaving you with the pot.

If you have a high hand, it is sometimes better to feign uncertainty, to draw other players in and get them to put in their chips.

If you are too cocky, it is likely everyone will fold and you won't be left with as big a pot as you hoped for.

Scoring

Poker hands are made up of five cards. They are ranked here, from highest (straight flush) to lowest (high card):

- Straight flush

  Five cards in suit and sequence – a royal flush (10, J, Q, K, A) beats any other hand

- Four of a kind

  Four cards of the same value plus any other card

- Full house

    Three of a kind and a pair of another kind

- Flush

    Five cards of the same suit but not in sequence

- Straight

    Five cards in sequence of rank but of different suits

- Three of a kind

    Three cards of the same value plus any two others

- Two pairs

    Two sets of two cards of the same value plus any other card

- Pair

    One set of two of the same value plus any three other cards

- High card to a hand that is none of the ones listed above. If none of the players have one of the hands listed above, then the highest card wins. If there is a tie for highest, then the next highest card wins.

High card

Offer intelligent insults

Don't insult people who will genuinely get offended. If you make someone run off sobbing, you'll just end up looking like a moron and no one will like you. When used in the right manner though, insults can be hilarious, especially when employed in a back-and-forth manner with your friends. The secret of being a good insulter is quick wit. You need to be able to come up with a great and unexpected quip in response to something someone has just said.

What you do

If you want to imply that someone is stupid, try:

- When God was throwing intelligence down from heaven, you must have had your umbrella up.

- A thought crossed your mind? It must have been a lonely journey.

- Calling you stupid would be an insult to stupid people.

- If I ever needed a brain transplant, I'd choose yours because I'd want one that hasn't been used.

- I refuse to have a battle of wits with an unarmed person.

If you want to imply they are boring:

- Please keep talking; I always close my eyes and snore when I'm interested.

- I hear everything you're saying; I just don't care.

- Don't you need a licence to be that boring?

- Sorry I drifted off there – I was just trying to imagine you with a personality.

If you want to imply they are ugly:

- Have you ever thought about suing your parents for giving you that face?

- I hope you don't mind if I take my glasses off when I talk to you; it's more pleasant.

- How come you're wearing a Frankenstein mask? Is there a dress-up party on?

- How come you're here? I thought they closed the zoo at night!

- You certainly hit every branch when you fell out of the ugly tree, didn't you?

Did you know?

A famous insult ...
Lady Astor to Winston Churchill: If I were your wife, I would poison your coffee.
Winston Churchill: Madam, if I were your husband, I would drink it.

Write a detective story

Detective novels are among the most popular fiction books. They follow a genre, which means that all of the stories work on similar principles. For example, there is always a crime, and someone out to solve it. There is a distinct formula for the detective genre and once you know it, you can follow it each time you want to write a detective story (Agatha Christie did!). Read a couple of detective stories and you'll find that each of them includes the following elements. Then you can write your own!

What you do

1 | The crime

A crime (usually a murder) has occurred. It has been committed by a villain who has not yet been discovered.

Arthur Binks, a millionaire, was killed with an ornamental knife during his 60th birthday celebration. He was discovered alone, dead in the library. The party took place at his summer home and the guests included his two daughters, Lily and Nina; his young wife, Helen (the daughters' stepmother); his golf partner, Pierre X; and Pierre's wife, Roberta X.

2 | The detective

A detective arrives to solve the crime. A detective may be male or female; they could be a lawyer or policeman, or a tough-talking private investigator, or a sharp-witted amateur (such as a nosey old lady).

A private investigator is hired by Helen Binks. The investigator is Michael Borlotti. Borlotti is quick-witted and has a habit of flipping a coin. He doesn't fit in among these rich folks and he isn't afraid to ask tough questions – he's here to do his job.

3 | The investigation

The detective conducts the investigation through solving or interpreting a series of clues. The detective should be smart and savvy, able to solve clues through sound reasoning and, sometimes, instinct.

Borlotti starts to uncover clues – it seems that Binks was not well-liked. Even his golf partner Pierre describes him as "a weasel." Everyone thinks that Helen married him for his money. Lily and Nina hate their stepmother and blame her for their father's death. But Borlotti is interested in the mysterious Roberta, the distant and alluring wife of Binks' friend Pierre X.

4 | The setting

Setting is important in detective novels and is described in detail. Often we are introduced to a dark and rainy city, full of shadow and crime. Sometimes we can find ourselves in grand old mansions where crimes take place behind doors.

The Binks mansion is beautiful and old, but full of secrets. The garden is particularly scary, overgrown, wild, and unnaturally still. Bonnie, Arthur Binks' pet cat, lurks in corners, hissing and meowing ominiously.

5 | Suspense

There is a sense of danger present, and readers will no doubt feel suspense as they follow the detective on the investigation. The detective will carefully explore mysterious places, where armed villains may be lurking. Throughout the story, the detective will gather clues from places where other people fail to look. The detective might notice a misplaced object that will prove to be invaluable in the future.

Borlotti doesn't seem to be making any progress. All the clues he has found have proved to be wild-goose chases. Everyone in the house seems to suspect Helen Binks, who is growing more moody by the day. Something seems to draw Borlotti to the garden. He walks up to it and realizes that there is something lurking in the shadows. Just when we think he is done for, Bonnie the cat leaps out of the bushes and runs away wildly. Borlotti looks closely at where the cat has sprung from and finds the key to the mystery.

6 | Ending

A detective story will end once the detective has gathered enough clues, talked to enough people, and managed to interpret the clues correctly. Often, suspects are gathered around as the detective reveals the mystery of the crime and the villain is exposed and brought to justice.

Borlotti gathers the suspects at the scene of the crime, the library. He slowly unveils the clues. He reveals the object he found in the garden – a comb from the hair of Roberta X! We discover that Roberta killed Binks as he was blackmailing her, threatening to reveal her dangerous past as a spy. To everyone's shock, Roberta breaks down, admitting her guilt, and she is apprehended by the local police.

Make a printing press

Have you ever wondered how to copy a newspaper article without using a printer or scanner? Well, if the electricity goes down
and all your modern-day tools are rendered useless and you really need that photocopy, you may just find you need an old-fashioned printing press. This activity involves the use of poisonous materials, so children will need adult supervision.

What you need

- A cup of water
- Half a cup of turpentine
- A few squirts of dishwashing liquid
- A glass jar
- A brush
- A plastic sheet
- Some A4 paper
- A piece of wood bigger than an A4 piece of paper

What you do

1 | First, you need to mix up the water, turpentine, and dishwashing liquid in the jar. This will be the ink for your printing press.

2 | Now you need to put the newspaper (the one you want to copy) on top of the plastic sheet of paper, which is laid out on a flat surface, such as a hard floor.

3 | With your brush, use the ink you have made to brush over the newspaper.

4 | Put a piece of A4 paper over the newspaper and then put the wood on top of it. Don't move the wood around or you will smudge the ink underneath.

5 | Press down on the wood with the heavy weight (for example, your body).

6 | Take the piece of wood off and take off the A4 paper. You should have a reverse copy of the newspaper article on your piece of A4 paper.

7 | To make a nonreverse copy of this paper, you need to let it dry.

8 | Now, instead of using the original newspaper, use your reverse copy and repeat the whole process (put ink over the top of it, an A4 sheet of paper, and the wood on top).

9 | Once you peel the new sheet of A4 paper back, you will have a copy of your original newspaper article!

Form and lead a club

So you're finally ready to form that Dachshund Appreciation Club you've always wanted. However, before you call your first meeting, you should make sure that you have a couple of things organized and under control.

What you do

1 | You need to write a list of objectives for your club.

- To organize a minimum of five dachshund-themed events per year.

- To provide a discussion forum for those interested in dachshunds and their welfare.

- To watch DVDs about dachshunds followed by a discussion forum.

2 | If your club is about an endangered species, such as the wedge-tailed eagle, or a venue that is about to close down, perhaps you need to organize fund-raising events that will raise awareness for your cause.

3 | Find some members.

- You need to find people who are interested in joining your club.

- If you have some friends who are as passionate about dachshunds as you are, then you've got a club. A club that involves just you and a lot of pictures of dachshunds isn't actually a club.

- Make sure that your club members agree with your club objectives and that they are willing and available to take part in club activities, such as meetings and events.

4 | Write a constitution, manifesto, or other document that your club members and you will abide by and with which you all agree. Make sure that all your members have signed it.

- We, the members of Dachshund Appreciation Club, are committed to the sharing of ideas, discussions, and anecdotes related to dachshunds. We will meet once a week to discuss dachshund-related issues and we will follow our objectives.

5   Now that you have the technicalities out of the way, you can do the fun stuff. Design a logo and make stickers, badges, T-shirts, and so on.

6   Once everything is ready, you can make a schedule and commence your meetings and club activities. Allow members to contribute ideas as to how your club can grow and achieve your objectives.

Win an argument

One of the most annoying things in life is to be out-argued by someone. Even though you know you are right, you end up mumbling something under your breath, red in the face, while your opponent brings you down with a carefully constructed point. If you know how to construct an argument and debate with someone, you are more likely to avoid this. There are a couple of things all arguers should keep in mind.

What you do

1   Know **your** argument.

   • Make sure that you have researched your argument well – don't argue about something you know nothing about.

   • You need to be aware of the issues involved in your argument so that you are not taken off guard by your opponent.

My argument is that the death penalty should not be introduced. I have researched this topic and am aware of the issues associated with it. My main arguments are: there is always room for error and the possibility that the wrong person will be executed; the death penalty is barbaric; humans should not be allowed to take the lives of others – it makes us as bad as murderers; the death penalty has not proved to be a deterrent to violent crimes.

2   Know **their** argument.

- Be aware of your opponent's side of the argument. That way, you can think up rebuttals and bring their point down.

My opponent believes that the death penalty should be introduced. Her main arguments are: some criminals cannot be rehabilitated and should be put to death; taxpayers should not have to give money to the upkeep of such criminals for the rest of their lives; it is a crime deterrent to potential offenders.

3   Be clear.

- Structure your argument clearly.

- If your argument is complex, make sure that you express it in a way that can be understood by others. You should employ logic and rationality when presenting your side of the argument.

4   Give evidence.

- If your argument is supported by evidence, make sure you use this. There is nothing like having some cold hard facts on your side.

Regions A and B have used the death penalty. Their crime rate is no lower than the neighboring regions Y and Z, which do not have the death penalty.

5 | Don't get emotional.

- Getting emotional can be a big problem. For people to believe your argument, they need to think you are a rational person, not someone who has a personal stake in the argument. As soon as emotions get into it, your credibility will leave you.

- Make sure you avoid emotionally charged phrases or arguments against your opponent – it goes against the rationality you are trying to maintain. "I can't believe you want to kill people," or "You are as bad as the murderers," is not the right way to go. It is better to say something like: "Aren't we as a society just as cruel if we allow the murder of murderers? Isn't that condoning a despicable act?"

6 | Be polite.

- People will respect you more if you show them respect.

- You are not out to make your opponent feel inferior; you just have opposing viewpoints on an argument. If there is an audience present, they will admire your polite attitude and will be inclined to support you.

- It is nice to say something like: "I really enjoy discussing this complex issue that we are both passionate about."

Sell stuff

Instead of throwing out your unwanted stuff, you might want to organize a garage sale and make a little pocket change, as well as making some bargain hounds happy.

What you need

- Cardboard for making signs
- Thick markers
- A table or improvised "counter"

- A tin full of change
- Lots of unwanted stuff (not rubbish)
- Labels

What you do

1 | Make some good signs advertising your sale.

- Use color.

- Include appropriate information – the location and, if appropriate, the kind of goods you are selling ("lots of 50s-style clothes!" or "backyard furniture!").

- Specify the time of your sale.

- Place the signs in appropriate spots (close to the location of the sale, where they will be seen by as many people as possible).

2 | Make sure you have good things to sell. Perhaps you could make a joint sale with a friend or neighbor. Also, ensure that the things you are selling are in working order and of appropriate quality.

3 | Arrange things in a suitable manner.

- Make your sale attractive and easily accessible.

- Put desirable items on display.

- Do not hide items so they can't be seen.

- Put similar things together. For example, have a clothes rack beside a box with hats in it. Keep the children's toys together, and special-interest items (your late aunt's taxidermy collection) all together.

4 | Label your items with price tags. Be reasonable. Even if you think your Grease soundtrack cassette tape is worth a lot, no one will buy it for more than a dollar or two.

5 | Be polite to your customers when they arrive, and be prepared to haggle and bargain. Remember, you want to get rid of your things, so you may have to lower the price on some items.

Put on a great party

To put on a great party, you need to plan ahead. Here are some tips that will ensure a smooth and fun time for all.

What you do

1. Send out invitations.

   - Do this well in advance (a few weeks) so that people have time to prepare and clear their schedules.

   - Include all necessary details such as reason for the party (your birthday), time, place, theme (if any), and dress code (if any).

2. Consider a themed party. Don't make the theme too narrow, or people will struggle to find a costume. Some successful past party themes have included:

   - Letter themes (if your name begins with S, maybe you can have an S party and your party will be populated by sea horses, shoeshines, and secretaries)

   - Horror

   - Pajamas

   - Time warp (the sixties, the nineties)

   - Science fiction

   - Pirates

   - Villains and heroes

3. Prepare some interesting food. Make sure you have a mix of snacks that cater to all your guests. Keep in mind food preferences (vegetarians, allergies) and make sure you have some healthy snacks to go with the unhealthy ones. You can always do something exciting with food, without too much effort.

   - You might decide to serve only red food. You can serve red cordial, red orange juice, strawberries, cherries, red licorice, tomato sandwiches, and peppers with beetroot dip.

   - Food coloring can also be fun. Red macaroni with tomato sauce or red rice with beetroot can look very impressive.

- If you are having a horror-themed party, you can make food look particularly morbid by using blue coloring, or questionable-looking ingredients. People have been known to make cocktail frankfurters with sauce look like severed fingers; others have stuck incredibly realistic insects around the table. If you dim the lights and serve grapes that have been secretly peeled, people will no doubt shriek with disgust at the unexpected eyeball-ish texture.

4 | Be a good host when your guests arrive. You need to make your guests feel comfortable by being a relaxed and happy host. If people don't know each other, try to introduce people who you think would get along.

5 | Play some party games. The important thing to keep in mind is that games are fun, but don't force people into them. Sometimes it's good to wait for people to get settled and relaxed before starting with the party play!

- Simple name game: get everyone standing in a circle. Each person must say their name, and a quality that describes them, beginning with the same letter. Who knows, Hesitant Harry might become great friends with Bewildered Ben.

- Scavenger hunt

- Truth or dare

- Charades

- Blind man's bluff

- Spin the bottle

- Pin the tail on the donkey

- Musical chairs

6 | It is polite to send thank-you letters after your party, especially if people have brought you presents. If you can remember who gave you what, you can thank people for their attendance as well as the present they got you.

Dance

If you know some basics, there's no excuse not to do it. Most people find dancing fun, and it's a pity that some people avoid it just because they feel uncomfortable. Remember – before anything, dancing should be an enjoyable activity. Here are some pointers that you can practice on your own and then employ at most parties.

What you need

- Music
- Your body

What you do

1 | Listen to the music and try to pick up the rhythm. Often you can find the rhythm by counting to four, or three in your head, along with the music.

2 | Stand naturally. You can hold your hands by your sides, or on your hips. Or you might be holding a snack or drink.

3 | Bob your head. This is a good start as people will think you are enjoying yourself and appreciating the music. You can bob your head to the count (four times in four beats) or once every two beats for a more casual bob. If you don't like bobbing your head, you might like to shrug your shoulders up and down, or move your hips a little. It doesn't hurt to look around and see how other people are enjoying the music – you may be inspired.

4 | Start moving side to side. You don't need to move your feet, you might like to shift your body weight, do a little side-to-side with your hips, or even move your shoulders right to left, with your hips following. Or you can move your knees bending one, then the other, to shift your weight. Practice doing this to the rhythm. It may be best to shift weight from one side to the other every second beat.

5 | Start to lift your feet off the ground. You can take little shuffling steps that follow your side-to-side body movement. Or you can take larger steps, whatever you feel comfortable with. Keep your body relaxed and moving. Your shoulders can be loose. If you don't feel comfortable lifting your feet, just drift your body from side to side and focus your attention back on your enjoyment of the music.

6 | If you haven't already done so, try to make your body flow with your movement. Let your hips move from side to side, following the direction of your feet. You can experiment with twisting your body, moving your shoulders, your arms, your legs, or whatever feels right.

7 | If you are feeling really comfortable dancing, feel free to elaborate. You can move your arms at chest height, holding loose fists as if you are a train steaming ahead. You might like to put your arms in the air. You can swing them around and do a corkscrew motion with your body, or you can pump them up and down as if you are a weight lifter or a cheering fan. Remember to keep your shoulders relaxed, and it is fine to stop if you begin to feel uncomfortable, or if the ecstatic "moment" that made you raise your arms has passed.

8 | Experiment. Dance in front of the mirror, with young children, with pets, and with friends. Dancing doesn't have to be serious. Do some silly dancing to make yourself feel comfortable.

Get messy with do-it-yourself paintball

Paintball is an extremely easy, fun, and safe sport – yet you get to throw exploding paintballs at your friends, get very dirty, and act totally crazy.

Paintball is usually played at venues and involves the use of paintball guns and gelatine paintballs. This version is an improvised form of paintball, which uses paint "bombs" and can be played with friends in a park or another outdoor area. A warning – this game is very, very messy. You will almost certainly end up covered in paint.

What you need

- Two teams of people

- Water bomb balloons

- Clothes that can be thrown out afterward

- Water-based liquid children's paint with nontoxic pigments in two colors (one for each team)

- A basket for each player (or another vessel in which to carry the bombs)

What you do

1 | Fill the water bombs with paint. Give each player the same number of bombs.

2 | Split up into teams.

3 | Play! All paintball games operate on the same principle: you must run around like mad, hide from the opposing team, and ruthlessly hunt down your enemies. Once you are hit with a paintball, you are eliminated from the game. Pretty messy – and very fun!

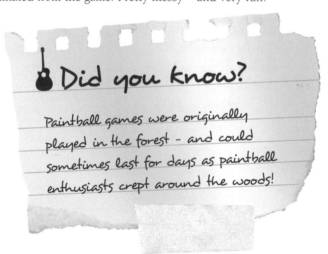

Did you know?

Paintball games were originally played in the forest – and could sometimes last for days as paintball enthusiasts crept around the woods!

Variations

- Elimination: Your team must get rid of all the opposing team members. The surviving team wins.

- Capture the flag: The teams compete to get a flag, and raise it at their team's flag station.

- King of the hill: Teams compete to capture a base (or bases). The winning team is the one that captures the base for the longest period of time. Once you are hit with a paintball, you are eliminated from the game.

Play the guitar

Guitar players can dazzle an audience with a great rock, flamenco, or blues performance. Or they can come in handy when you're sitting around with a bunch of friends singing old favorites at the top of your lungs. To be a good guitar player, you need to spend years practicing your art. But here are some basics to get you started.

What you need

- An acoustic guitar

What you do

1   Make sure you have correct posture. You should never be tense or in pain. Notice how the guitar shape is usually designed with the human body in mind. The curvature of the guitar body allows the guitar to sit comfortably on your thigh, and the neck is scaled so that your left arm (right arm if you are left handed) is free to move up and down the guitar with ease.

2   This is how your left hand should be positioned. (Right hand if you are left handed.)

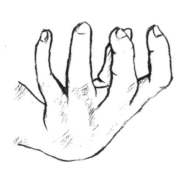  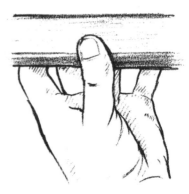

3   Have your thumb centered on the back of the guitar neck and relatively straight. Your fingers should be curved and straight. This creates what is commonly referred to as "the claw" grip, with the second and third fingers touching the thumb (the claw).

4 | To hold the plectrum (pick), you need to:

- Put your hand out as if you are going to do a karate chop.

- Bend your index finger inward as far as it comfortably goes.

- Sit the plectrum between the outside of your index finger and your thumb.

5 | The plectrum should look as though it is coming out of the side of your thumb. The remaining fingers should be outstretched and relaxed. The pressure you apply to the plectrum should be minimal – try not to tense up when you play!

6 | The first three pictures demonstate how to hold the plectrum. The fourth picture is simply a different view of the third picture.

7 | Now that you are set to play, you can start by reading guitar diagrams and playing some simple chords.

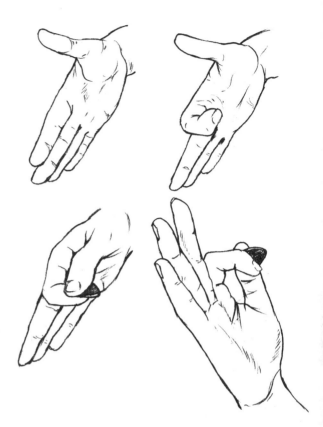

Understanding common guitar diagrams

There are two main types of diagrams that you will encounter when playing the guitar.

1 | Chord diagrams

These are pictures of the guitar neck with relevant information about which fret and what fingers to use. (A chord is more than one note played together at the same time – usually a minimum of three notes.)

- Chord diagrams are upright pictures of the guitar neck.

- The numbers represent which fingers you should use.

- The "X" means don't play this string. The "O" means play the string open.

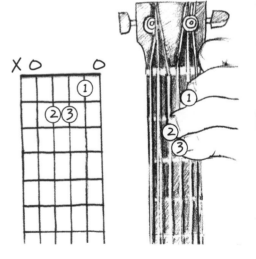

2 | Tablature

This is a visual guide showing where to put your fingers.

- Tablature is the easiest way to communicate music notation on the guitar.

- The lines represent the strings.

- The numbers represent the fret numbers you press on with your fingers.

- Sometimes a second set of smaller numbers is written underneath the fret numbers. These numbers would tell you which fingers to use.

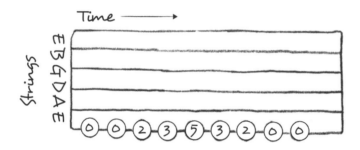

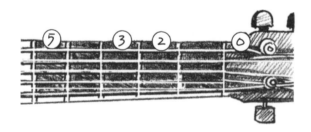

Basic chords

These are all the basic major and minor chords.

Major chords are happy sounding chords.

- A major
- C major
- D major
- E major
- G major

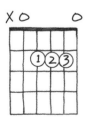
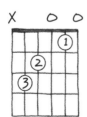
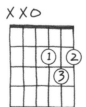
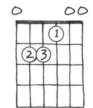
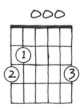

Minor chords are sad sounding chords.

- A minor
- D minor
- E minor

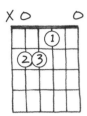 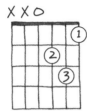 

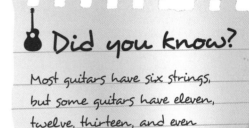

🎸 **Did you know?**

Most guitars have six strings, but some guitars have eleven, twelve, thirteen, and even eighteen strings!

Play!

Start practicing with an old favorite.

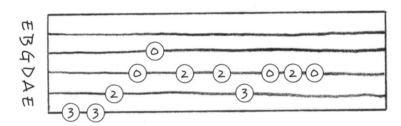

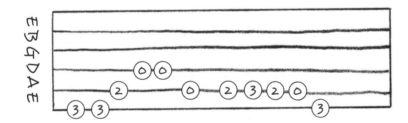

🎸 **Did you know?**

Stringed instruments similar to the guitar have been around for over 5000 years! It is thought the early guitar originated in Central Asia.

SCIENCE

Make lightning

Homemade lightning is easiest seen when it's dark.

What you need

- Nylon comb
- Woolen sweater or cloth
- Metal door knob or frame

Did you know?

Very clear and dry days are best for making lightning.

What you do

1 | Rapidly rub the comb on the woolen sweater or cloth for 30 seconds. The comb will gain an electrical charge.

2 | Bring the comb very, very close to the door handle or door frame, without touching it. You should see a spark jump the gap – like lightning jumping from the clouds to earth.

Grow crystals

Growing crystals is easy. Growing large, perfectly shaped single crystals takes longer and is much harder.

Your first aim is to make a "saturated solution" – which means that no more solid will dissolve at that temperature. When the solution cools or evaporates, the solid will be released. If this cooling or evaporation takes place slowly, nicely shaped crystals will result. If the cooling is quick, the crystals will be smaller and more jumbled.

What you need

- Epsom salts (from a supermarket or pharmacy)
- Warm water
- Clean glass jar with a screw lid
- A tablespoon

- A teaspoon
- A glass or jar with a flat bottom
- A magnifying glass
- Another wide glass jar or dish

What you do

1 | Put three tablespoons of warm (bath temperature) water into the small, clean glass jar that a lid will fit.

2 | Add two tablespoons of Epsom salts.

3 | Fit the lid and shake well.

4 | Rest the jar in the bowl of warm water for 5 minutes, and then shake it well again.

5 | If all the Epsom salts has dissolved, add another teaspoonful.

6 | Repeat steps 3–5, adding Epsom salts a teaspoonful at a time and shaking, until some remains at the bottom of the jar after the second shaking.

7 | Pour two or three drops of the clear liquid onto the flat bottom of an upturned glass or jar. Keep watching them through a magnifying glass. You should be able to watch the crystals grow almost immediately.

Variation

To make bigger and better crystals, pour the rest of the clear liquid into a shallow dish or an open-topped wide jar until it is about 1 cm (about 0.3 in) deep. Let it cool and dry up slowly. The longer it takes, the better the crystal shapes will be.

There are many things that control when you will see crystals start to grow. They can start to appear in an hour or two – or they may take several days, as the liquid dries up.

You should end up with needle-shaped crystals, much larger than the ones you started with.

(Thoroughly wash your hands and equipment. Epsom salts is a laxative!)

Extract DNA in your own kitchen

DNA is present in every living part of every living thing. It contains the unique code for the individual's looks and functioning.

What you need

- 150 g (6 oz) of broccoli florets (or onion)
- Large pinch of salt (not more)
- Cold water
- Blender
- Fine sieve or strainer
- Measuring jug

- Liquid detergent
- ("Meat tenderizer" powder or fresh pineapple juice. Optional extra.)
- Rubbing alcohol (60–95% ethyl or isopropyl alcohol)
- Small narrow glass jar or bottle

What you do

1 Chop the broccoli or onion so that it fits in the blender. Add a cup of cold water and a large pinch of salt.

2 Blend at high speed for 25–30 seconds.

3 Strain the "soup" through a sieve and into a measuring jug. Press the solid gently, if necessary, until you have half a cup of "juice."

4   Add one tablespoon of liquid detergent to the juice. (An added pinch of meat tenderizing powder (enzyme), or a tablespoon of fresh pineapple juice, may produce a larger amount of DNA – but is not essential.) Stir gently for five seconds.

5   Leave it to rest for 10 minutes.

6   Pour the liquid into a small, narrow glass jar or bottle so that it's about one-third full.

7   Tilt it to one side as you trickle an equal volume of alcohol down the side, and then set it upright and let it rest again. The alcohol will float on the top.

8   The DNA clumps together in stringy strands that rise into the alcohol almost immediately. They can be hooked out with a cocktail stick, or similar.

Suck an egg into a bottle

What you need

- A hard-boiled egg (or a soft-boiled one if you don't mind the mess)

- A large bottle with a smooth top slightly smaller than the egg

- Large bowl or bucket of hot water

- Large bowl or bucket of cold water with ice in it

What you do

1   Peel the shell off the egg.

2   Wipe the top of the bottle and the inside of the neck with liquid detergent (to make it slippery and create an airtight seal).

3   Hold most of the bottle in the hot water for 5 minutes, without letting water enter (to heat the air inside).

4   Place the egg on the top of the bottle and plunge the bottle into the ice-cold water and keep it there. The air inside will shrink and the egg will be "sucked" in.

5   To remove the egg, blow hard into the bottle. Keep blowing while you tilt the bottle until the egg rests on the opening. Take your mouth away while the egg shoots out.

Variation

If you have a glass bottle, here's another way
(with adult help):

1 | Fold a strip of paper (about 5 cm (2 in) wide and
  | 15 cm (6 in) long) in half lengthways.

2 | Set light to the paper as you drop it into
  | the bottle.

3 | Immediately place the egg on top.

4 | The flames will soon go out after the burning paper has heated the air and used up the oxygen.
  | When the air cools, the egg will be "sucked" in (actually, pushed in by the extra air pressure on
  | the outside).

Tip

*When you want to get the
egg out, shake out the burnt
paper before blowing into
the bottle!*

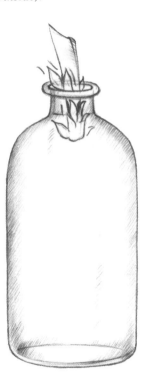

Make an electromagnet

When electricity passes through a wire, it creates magnetism around it. To make the magnetism stronger, you can coil the wire, wrap the coils around something made of iron or steel, increase the number of coils, or increase the flow of electricity – or do all of these.

What you need

- A fresh C-cell battery

- About 1 m (3 ft) of thin wire with a plastic insulation covering

- A large, thick steel screw about 8 cm (3 in) long

- Wire cutters or old scissors

- Sticky tape (optional)

- Metal paper clips

Tip

Try to connect the battery for only five or six seconds at a time, or it will soon run out of energy. To make the magnet even stronger, you can use a 9-volt battery.

What you do

1. Remove the insulation from each end of the wire so that there are enough exposed metal strands to hold on to each end of the battery.

2. Leave about 10 cm (4 in) of wire, and then start wrapping about 20 tight and close loops around the screw, starting at one end and working toward the other.

3. Hold them in place with the tape, if you wish.

4. Keep wrapping more coils around the screw, over the top of the first ones, working your way back toward where you started.

5. See how many paper clips will attach to the end of the screw before and after you connect the bare ends of the wire to the battery.

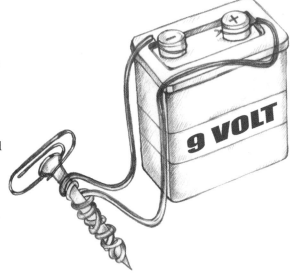

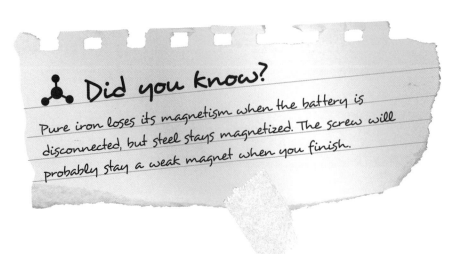

Did you know?

Pure iron loses its magnetism when the battery is disconnected, but steel stays magnetized. The screw will probably stay a weak magnet when you finish.

Make an empty can implode

What you need

- An empty aluminum ring-pull drink can
- A pair of kitchen tongs
- A large bowl or half a sink full of cold water
- A tablespoon
- A cooktop

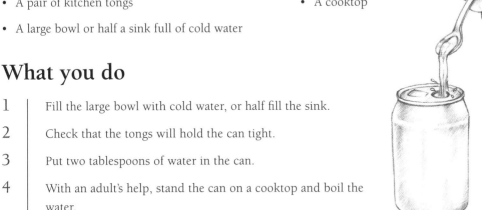

What you do

1. Fill the large bowl with cold water, or half fill the sink.
2. Check that the tongs will hold the can tight.
3. Put two tablespoons of water in the can.
4. With an adult's help, stand the can on a cooktop and boil the water.
5. When steam has come out of the can for 20 seconds, with the palm of your hand pointing upward, grip the can with the tongs.
6. Quickly take the can to the cold water, turn it up side down (be very careful not to tip boiling water on yourself) and keep the top of the can below the cold water level.
7. Watch what happens!

How it works

The steam pushes the air out of the can. When the can cools, the steam turns back to a small amount of water. The air pressure outside will squeeze the can inward and, without air inside to push back, this pressure will "implode" the can.

Did you know?

Air pressure is greater than you think – just watch the can collapse!

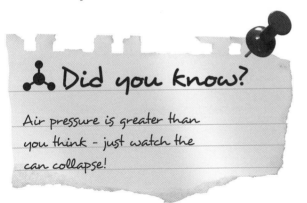

Grow plants on cotton balls

Seeds need air, moisture, and a suitable temperature to grow. They won't grow if they stay underwater for a long time. The seeds of some plants, such as alfalfa, cress, and mustard (all of which you can eat when they sprout), and flowers like Virginia Stock, will grow if they are sprinkled on moistened cotton balls.

What you need

- Jar or clear plastic drinking cup
- Water
- Seeds
- Cotton balls
- Cloth or paper towel and elastic band

Did you know?

Small plants will grow for a long time on cotton balls, and may even flower. Alfalfa seeds will sprout in about two days. The tops can be eaten when they are about 3 cm (1 in) high, and green.

What you do

1 | Pour about 5 mm (a little less than 0.25 in) of warm water into the jar or drinking cup.

2 | Soak cotton balls in warm water, and then gently squeeze most of the water out.

3 | Add two layers of moistened cotton balls to the container.

4 | After 10 minutes, pour as much water out of the container as you can.

5 | Scatter your chosen seeds on top of the cotton balls.

6 | Cover the top of the container with fabric and fix it in place with an elastic band. This helps to keep the air and seeds moist.

7 | Put the container in a warm cupboard or dark place at about 15°C (60°F).

8 | As soon as the seeds sprout, place the container where it will get plenty of light. Some plants like being in the sun, but some don't – check the packet.

9 | After a few days, remove the cover. It's probably best to gradually put the seedlings in the sun longer and longer each day.

10 | Keep the cotton balls moist, but not under water.

Make a volcano

What you need

- Small, clean plastic or glass bottle with a narrow top, about 250 ml (8 oz) size
- Yeast
- Honey
- Tablespoon
- Flour
- Salt
- Cooking oil
- Water
- Large bowl
- Baking pan

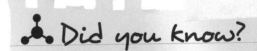

Did you know?

The bubbles in real volcano lava are filled with the same gas that makes the bubbles in this model.

What you do

1 | In the large bowl, use your hands to mix 6 cups of flour, 2 cups of salt, 4 tablespoonfuls of cooking oil, and 2 cups of water. Yes, it's "play dough"! You will use it for the sides of your volcano. You can add a little more water, if you need to, to make the dough stick together.

2 | Put two tablespoons of honey in the bottle. Half fill it with warm water and shake it until the honey dissolves.

3 | Add 2 tablespoonfuls of dried yeast and shake to mix.

4 | Fill the bottle with warm water.

5 | Stand the bottle in the middle of the baking tray.

6 | Quickly press the dough around the bottle to make a volcano shape, but try not to let any fall in. Slope the sides down from the top – no crater.

7 | When all is ready, put your volcano on something flat outside, where mess doesn't matter, or in the sink.

8 | Bubbles of "lava" will flow for several minutes.

Tip

This is a good thing to do outside, but if you are going to do it inside, make sure you choose a baking pan that fits inside the sink.

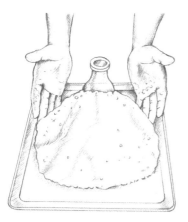

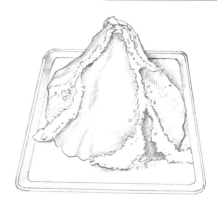

Measure acids and bases with red cabbage

An "indicator" is a chemical that changes color when an acid or an alkali is added to it. Alkali is the opposite of acid. "Bases" are substances that dissolve in water to make alkalis (alkaline solutions). Solutions that are neither acid nor alkali are "neutral." Pure water is neutral.

What you need

- Half a small red cabbage
- Grater
- Saucepan
- Water
- Strainer

- Scissors
- Paper towel or coffee filter paper
- Plate
- Small containers
- Liquids to test

What you do

1 | Grate or chop the red cabbage into the saucepan. Just cover it with water and boil for 20–30 minutes. The liquid will turn dark purple.

| 2 | Let the juice cool, and then strain it into a container. |

| 3 | Cut strips of paper towel or coffee filter paper about 5 cm (2 in) long. |

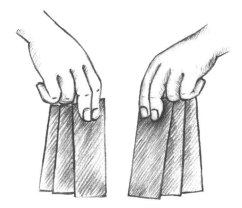

4	Soak them in the juice, and then lay them flat on the plate to dry.
5	Put each liquid you will test in a clean container (you only need a few drops).
6	Dip a new dry "indicator paper" strip into each one and see what color the paper turns.

| 7 | The indicator paper turns red or yellow in acids, green in neutral solutions, and blue/green to purple in alkalis. |

Experiment

You cannot use this indicator to test colored substances, like ink!

Some suggestions for substances you can test are:

- Lemon

- Orange and other fruit juices

- Milk
- Baking soda in water
- Dishwashing detergent/shampoo/laundry detergent/soap in water
- Toothpaste in water
- Fizzy drinks
- Vinegar

Lemon   Orange   Vinegar   Milk   Tap water   Soda water

Charm worms

If you get good at this, there are worm charming competitions that you can enter. The idea is to make worms wriggle out of the ground without digging or pouring on water or chemicals. One champion managed to charm 511 out of a 3 m² (3 yd²) area in half an hour.

What you do

Favorite competition methods include:

1 | Jump up and down on the ground.

2 | Play music.

3 | Push garden fork prongs about 15 cm (6 in) into the soil, and then make them vibrate and ring by hitting them or rubbing them with a stick with notches on it. Experts tune their forks by filing them and make special beating or rubbing tools.

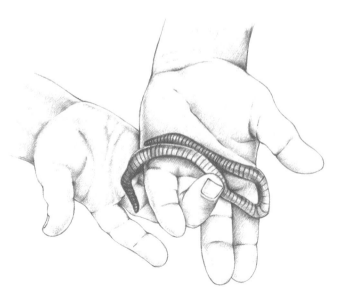

4 | Experiment with:

- A range of fork sizes to provide different notes.

- Pushing the prongs to different depths.

- Hitting the prongs with different objects to produce new tones.

- The number of forks added to the soil in a given area, and therefore the spacing between them.

- Other things that could be hit to produce vibrations in the soil.

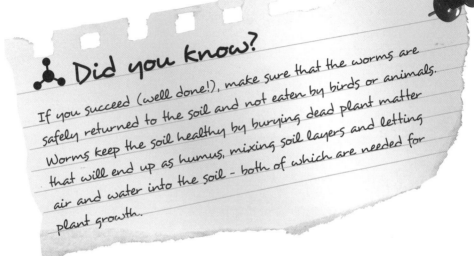

Did you know?

Worm charming is likely to work best at dusk in spring and autumn, when dew is on the ground and when the soil is moist.

Did you know?

If you succeed (well done!), make sure that the worms are safely returned to the soil and not eaten by birds or animals. Worms keep the soil healthy by burying dead plant matter that will end up as humus, mixing soil layers and letting air and water into the soil – both of which are needed for plant growth.

Make long-life soap bubbles

Bubbles often burst when they touch dry things. If you stand a drinking cup or glass upside down and wet the bottom with bubble mixture, a bubble blown with a straw will sit on top for a long time. When you wet the inside and outside of the straw with bubble mixture, you can push it into the bubble and blow another small bubble inside the first one.

What you need

- Bubble mixture (from a toy store)

- Water

- Glycerin

- Jar with a screw lid that makes a good seal

- Drinking straw

- Something glass or plastic that's curved like part of a ball (optional)

What you do

1 | Mix equal quantities of bubble mixture, water, and glycerin.

2 | Let the new mixture stand overnight.

3 | Coat the inside of the jar and the lid with the new mixture.

4 | Use the straw and new mixture to blow a bubble inside the jar, and then seal it with the lid. Sometimes the bubble will last for weeks!

5 | The bubble will last longest if you can use bubble mixture to wet something curved in the jar for it to sit in – for example, an old lens from a pair of glasses or a hollow dome-shaped piece of plastic cut from some packaging.

Tip

As manufacturers make bubble mixture in a wide variety of strengths, you need to experiment. Try a different combination of ingredients each time you make "long-life mixture" and see what quantity works best.

Did you know?

You can increase the time bubbles last by adding glycerin to bubble mixture.

Walk on liquid

What you need

- Large plastic ice-cream tub (or similar) that your foot will fit in

- Four cups of cornstarch

- Mixing spoon

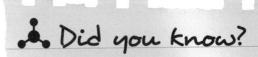

Did you know?

"Isotropy" is the scientific word that describes liquids that become solids when they are moved. They are "isotropic."

What you do

1 | Put the cornstarch in the tub.

2 | Add cold water gradually, while stirring. Slowly rub the powder against the tub side with the spoon until the crumbs stick together, like a paste. When you stop stirring, or slow down, you will see liquid on the top.

3 | If you squeeze or rub the paste with your hands, it becomes firm and dry; but when you stop, it will run through your fingers as a liquid.

4 | If you step on the mixture quickly (barefoot!) while walking, it will take your weight and be solid – but if you walk slowly or stand still, you will sink in liquid. (You can punch the mixture, to test it, before you walk.)

⚛ Did you know?

The same thing happens on some wet sandy beaches. The sand stays firm while you keep walking; but when you stop, your feet start to sink below the surface.

⚛ Did you know?

Tomato sauce (ketchup) is the opposite. It's "thixotropic." When you shake the bottle or hit the end, the sauce becomes runnier.

Dissolve a tooth in Coke

Does it disappear? How long does it take? You may have heard that this happens. Now is the time to be a scientist and put Coke to the test!

It's true that Coke does contain a mixture of acids, including phosphoric acid, but other things we eat and drink contain acids, too.

- Milk – lactic acid

- Vinegar – acetic acid

- Orange juice – citric acid

- Soda water – carbonic acid

… and Coke and all these liquids contain water. If you are going to test all these liquids for their dissolving power, you should test plain water, too.

How long does it take any of these to dissolve teeth? Or eggshells? Or nails made of steel?

What you need

- Same-sized containers

- Same amounts of each test liquid

- Same-sized iron nails

- Same-sized squares, circles (draw around a coin), or triangles of boiled eggshell

- Magnifying glass

Did you know?

You will probably find that Coke does not dissolve things much faster than other acid foods and drinks. It won't dissolve the nail in four days, as some people will tell you.

Did you know?

If you have teeth that fall out, boil them in some water before adding them to test liquids. It is only fair to compare the time it takes Coke to dissolve a tooth with the time other liquids take. It will take a very long time before a tooth dissolves!

What you do

1 | Set up your containers of test liquids and leave them overnight so that they are all the same temperature.

2 | If you are using boiled eggshells, after they have been cut with scissors, try to remove the "skin" from the inside.

3 | Add in your test solids (put the eggshell and nails in separate containers).

4 | Remove the nails and the eggshells each day, wipe them, and look at them carefully with a magnifying glass. Note what you see.

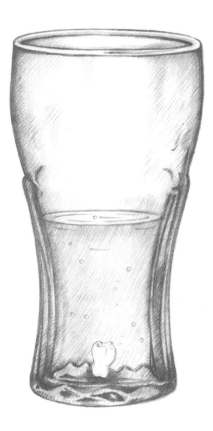

Color a rose blue

There are no rosebushes that will produce blue flowers naturally – but you can make roses change color.

What you need

- White rose with a stem – at least 20 cm (8 in) long

- Vase or jar

- Water

- Scissors

- Blue food coloring

Did you know?

You can try other food colors, too, or ink. You can also experiment with roses of different colors, but they won't turn pure blue.

What you do

1   If you cut a rose from a bush, or buy one from a store, put the end of the stem in water as soon as you can.

2   Fill the vase or jar with water. Add drops of food coloring until the water is bright blue.

3   Trim the stem at an angle so that it's about 15 cm (6 in) long, and immediately put the end in the blue water.

4   Watch what happens over the next two to three days.

Variation

Using a knife, you can split the stem in two lengthways and put one side in a jar with one food color and the other side in jar containing a different color.

Measure wind speed (anemometer)

An anemometer is a measuring tool for checking wind speed. Here's how you can make one.

What you need

- A protractor
- A matchstick, cocktail stick, kebab stick, or similar
- Sticky tape
- Sewing "cotton" or 1 kg (2 lb) nylon fishing line
- Standard-weight table tennis ball
- Needle

What you do

1. Use the needle to make two tiny holes in the table tennis ball, one opposite the other. This is easiest done by heating the tip of the needle in a flame.

2. Sew the cotton or fishing line thread through the ball, leaving about 45 cm (1 ft 6 in) on one side. Tie it tight and cut off any extra.

3. Tie the other end to the stick and wind the thread around the stick until the distance from the stick to the top of the ball is 30 cm (1 ft).

4. Use the sticky tape to attach the stick to the protractor. The thread should hang down from the outside, from the center point.

5. To measure the wind speed, line up the protractor with the wind direction. Hold it by the corner, as far from your body as possible. The thread should not touch the protractor.

6. When the wind speed is zero, the thread will hang straight down on the 90-degree mark. When it's blowing, read off the number of degrees and then check this table for the wind speed:

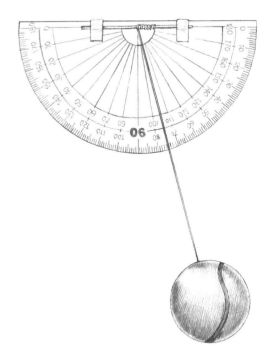

Degrees	Approximate wind speed (kilometers per hour)	Approximate wind speed (miles per hour)
90	0	0
85	10	6
77	15	9
70	20	12
58	25	15
48	30	18
40	35	21
33	40	24
27	45	27
23	50	30

Grow a stalactite

It takes hundreds of years for stalactites to grow from the roof of a cave, or stalagmites to grow upward from the floor. You can make your own in a few weeks, by the same process.

What you need

- Jars or glasses, the same size
- About 45 cm (18 in) of cotton string or wool
- Paper clips
- Saucer
- Epsom salts or baking soda
- Spoon

Did you know?

When the drips evaporate, they leave a little of the dissolved chemical behind. This is also what happens in caves. Because you dissolved a lot of chemical in the water, you should start to see a result in two to three weeks.

What you do

1 | Nearly fill both jars with hot water. Put them about 15 cm (6 in) apart.

2 | To each of them, add as much Epsom salts or baking soda as will dissolve.

3 | Tie paper clips to the ends of the string to weight them down.

4 | Soak the string in the solution, and then drape it from one jar to the other so that it sags in the middle.

5 | Put the saucer underneath to catch the drips.

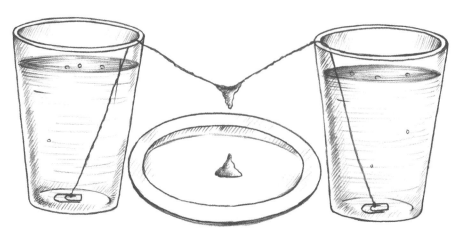

Bend water

What you need

- Nylon comb
- Woolen sweater or cloth

What you do

1. Turn on the tap gently until the drips just join to make a thin, steady flow.
2. Rub the back of a nylon comb on something woolen.
3. Hold the back of the comb vertically, and then bring it close to the water.
4. The water will bend toward the comb.

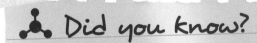

Did you know?

Water becomes electrically charged as it leaves a tap. It then becomes attracted to objects that are oppositely charged.

Did you know?

You can rub balloons and try other objects that are made of plastic, such as plastic bottles and polyethylene bags. Try other fabrics, too, especially those that are furry or silky.

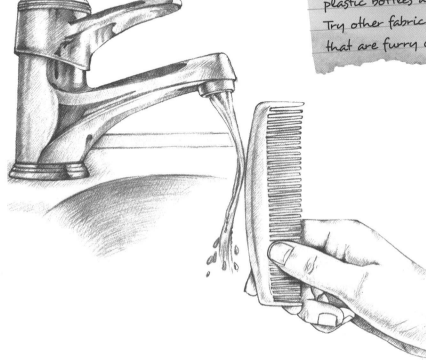

Clean silver the easy way

There's no need to spend hours polishing or using nasty chemicals to clean silver.

What you need

- Washing soda (sodium carbonate)
- China, Pyrex glass, or plastic bowl
- Aluminum foil
- Tablespoon
- Boiling water
- Measuring jug

What you do

1. Wash your silver item in soapy water to remove all grease.

2. Make a pad of two or three layers of aluminum foil at the bottom of the bowl.

3. Put a tablespoonful of washing soda in the middle of the foil and add just enough boiling water to cover the foil and dissolve the soda.

4. Put the silver item on the foil.

5. Add enough very hot water to cover the item, noting how much you add.

6. For every liter (quart) of water that you add, spoon in and dissolve an extra tablespoon of washing soda.

7. The silver should start to become bright again in about 30 seconds. While the item is on the foil and in liquid, use a soft brush to help remove old silver cleaner that's built up in nooks and crannies.

8. Rinse cleaned silver items in hot soapy water and dry them with a soft cloth.

9. Very black silver may need several treatments.

GADGETS

Make a battery

Do you want to make your own battery? With potatoes? Yes, that's right! Potatoes! Seriously. Here's how!

What you need

- Three fresh potatoes
- Three pieces of single-strand copper wire, 5 cm (2 in) long
- Three galvanized nails, 5 cm (2 in)
- Four alligator clip leads
- A light-emitting diode (LED)
- Sandpaper or steel wool

What you do

1	Scuff the nail and copper wire with the sandpaper or steel wool until they are shiny.
2	Push a nail and a piece of wire into the flat side of the potato about 2.5 cm (1 in). Make sure they don't touch – keep them 2.5 cm (1 in) or more apart. Repeat this step with the second and third potato. Let's call the potatoes A, B, and C.
3	Use an alligator clip lead to connect the copper wire of potato A to the positive (+) connection of the LED.
4	Use an alligator clip lead to connect the galvanized nail of potato C to the negative (−) connection of the LED.
5	Use an alligator clip lead to connect the galvanized nail of potato A to the copper wire of potato B.
6	Use an alligator clip lead to connect the galvanized nail of potato B to the copper wire of potato C.
7	That's it! As you connect the final lead, your LED should light up.

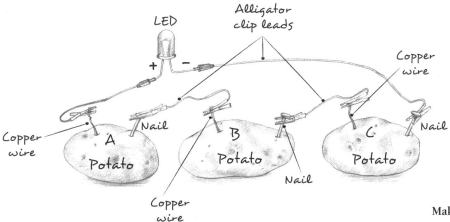

Further experiments

To see how much current your potato battery is making, get a digital or analog multimeter to measure the voltage or current of electricity (you can get one from an electronics shop). Replace the LED connected to your battery with the multimeter. How much current is your battery producing? Increase the size of your battery by adding more potatoes, and then measure the current again. Try some different fruit and vegetables and see if you can get the same amount of current from them.

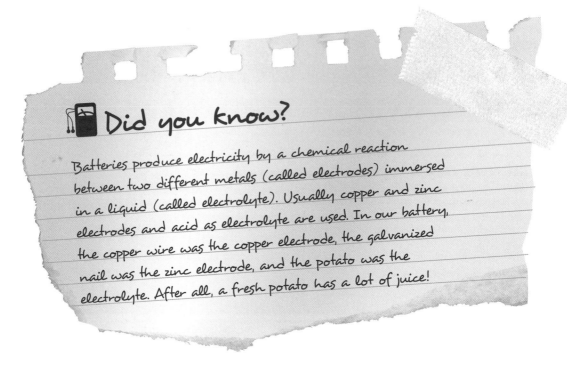

Did you know?

Batteries produce electricity by a chemical reaction between two different metals (called electrodes) immersed in a liquid (called electrolyte). Usually copper and zinc electrodes and acid as electrolyte are used. In our battery, the copper wire was the copper electrode, the galvanized nail was the zinc electrode, and the potato was the electrolyte. After all, a fresh potato has a lot of juice!

Make an electrical circuit

How does electricity from a battery make a light work? The electricity passes along a circuit to the light. Make your own circuit to see how this works.

What you need

- A battery with battery holder – if you don't have a battery holder, you can attach the wires with some electrical tape

- Three insulated wires with bare ends

- A small block of wood or cork

- Drawing pins

- A paper clip

- A three-volt flashlight bulb with holder (or you can use a buzzer)

What you do

1	Wind a bare wire end around a drawing pin. Hook the paper clip around the pin and press it into the wood block.
2	Wind the second bare wire end around another drawing pin and press it into the wood. Bend the paper clip up a little and press the second drawing pin into the wood block under the end of the paper clip. Your switch is now complete. It works by pressing the end of the paper clip down so that it touches the pin.

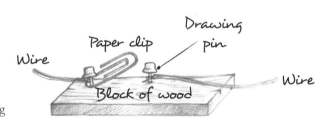

3	Attach the positive (+) side of the battery to the wire connected to the pin on your switch.
4	Attach the negative (−) side of the battery to a new wire.
5	Attach the other end of this wire to one point on the light bulb holder.
6	Onto the other point of the light bulb holder, attach the wire that is connected to the paper clip on your switch.
7	Your circuit is now ready for use. Press down on the paper clip. As it touches the pin, the circuit is closed, electricity flows through it, and the light bulb switches on.

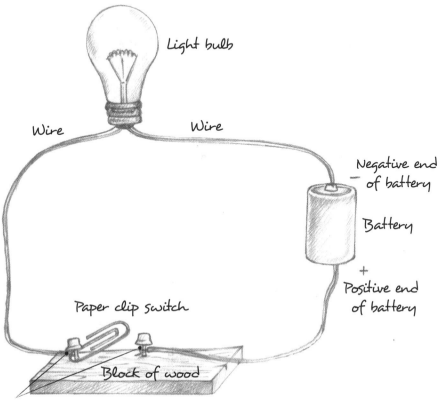

How it works

Electricity is the flow of electrons through a substance. Not all substances will allow electrons to flow – they are called insulators. Metals are generally good conductors of electricity and are used in wires. A circuit is the path formed by electric conductors.

Did you know?

The smallest battery in the world measures 2.9 mm in diameter and 13 mm in length (about the size of a pencil tip). It can, with recharging, last up to 10 years!

Build an electric motor

Electric motors are used to run all sorts of things, from toys to manufacturing equipment. You may think that they're really complex, but they're built on a very simple principle. You could even build your own simple electric motor with some household items.

What you need

- A D-cell battery
- A C-cell battery
- Metal safety pins
- A rubber band
- Insulated copper wire (1 m or about 3 ft)
- A magnet
- Some reusable adhesive putty (e.g., Blu-tack)
- A craft knife

What you do

1 | Wind the wire around the C-cell battery to form a tight coil. Make sure to leave about 5 cm (2 in) of straight wire at either end. (You don't have to use a C-cell battery for this, but it will produce the correct-size coil for your motor.)

2 | Carefully pull the coil off the battery, holding the wire so it doesn't spring out of shape. To make the coil hold its shape, wrap each free end of the wire around the coil a couple of times. Make sure that the new binding turns are exactly opposite each other so the coil can turn easily on the axis formed by the two free ends of the wire. (Or you could bind the coil with some electrical tape.)

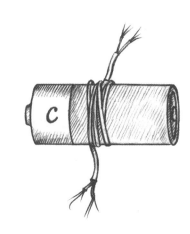

3 | With a craft knife (be careful), remove the top half of the insulation from the free wire at both ends. Be careful to leave the bottom half of the wire with the insulation intact. The top half of the wire will be shiny bare copper, and the bottom half will be the color of the insulation.

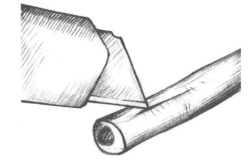

4 | Blu-tack the D-cell battery, lying horizontal, onto a flat surface.

5 | Use the rubber band to attach the two safety pins to either end of the battery. The top end of the safety pins should be pointing down and touching the positive (+) and negative (−) terminals of the battery. The bottom end of the safety pins should be pointing up and parallel.

6 | Insert the free wires from the coil into the loops at the bottom of the safety pins (which are pointing up). The coil should now be suspended over the battery. The coil should be centered between the safety pins. Give it a test spin to make sure it spins freely.

7 | Blu-tack the magnet onto the battery, right under the coil.

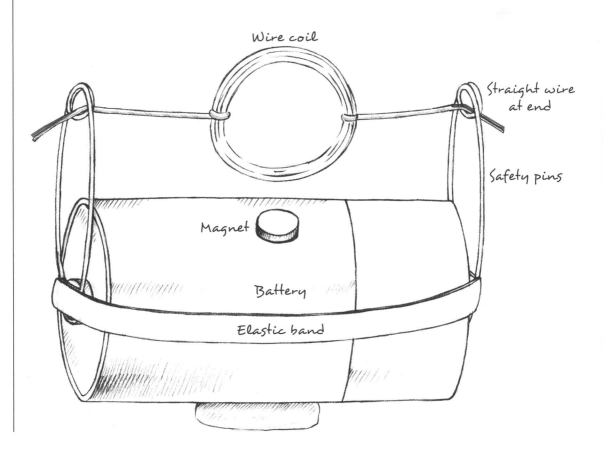

Wire coil

Straight wire at end

Safety pins

Magnet

Battery

Elastic band

8 | Spin the coil gently to get the motor started. If it doesn't start, try spinning it in the other direction. The motor will only spin in one direction. Once it starts, it will keep on spinning until the battery runs out of power. Turn the magnet upside down to make the coil spin in the other direction.

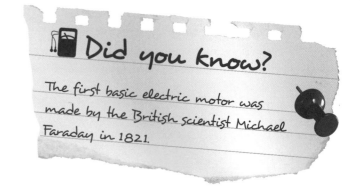

Did you know?

The first basic electric motor was made by the British scientist Michael Faraday in 1821.

Find north on your own compass

Which way is north? Point to it right now. If you can't, then use a compass to find out where north is. Do you have a compass? No? Don't worry – you can make one.

What you need

- A needle
- A bar magnet with a north and south pole
- A cork from a bottle
- A small bowl of water

Did you know?

The South Pole is the only point on Earth where all directions face north.

What you do

1 | Stroke the north pole of the magnet along the length of the needle, from head to point, at least 10 to 20 times. This will magnetize the needle.

2 | Cut off a small section from the end of the cork. About 10–12 mm will do (about half an inch).

3 | Drive the needle through the piece of cork, from one end of the circle to the other.

4 | Fill the bowl with water (half full will be enough). Float the cork and needle in the water.

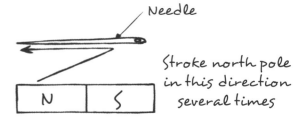

Needle

Stroke north pole in this direction several times

N	S

5 | Place your compass on a still surface and watch what happens. The point of the needle will face toward north.

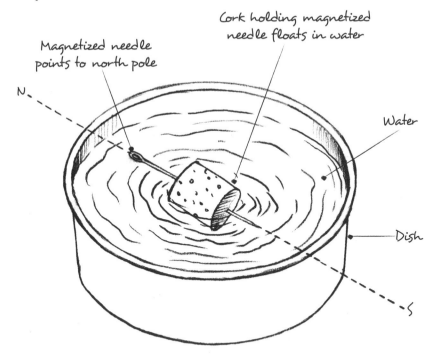

Cork holding magnetized needle floats in water

Magnetized needle points to north pole

N

Water

Dish

S

How it works

A magnet has the power to attract iron and steel and other magnets. A magnet has a north and south pole, and the north pole of one magnet and the south pole of another will attract each other. The core of the earth is rich in iron, so the Earth itself is like a magnet, with a north and south pole. The Earth's magnetic field is not strong enough to pull other magnets all the way to the South or North Pole, but it is strong enough to align other magnets.

By floating a magnetic needle on cork, it rotates freely and aligns with the Earth's magnetic poles.

Did you know?

Honeybees navigate by using the sun as a compass.

Did you know?

Bats use a magnetic substance in their body called magnetite as an "internal compass" to help them navigate.

Stargaze through a homemade telescope

A telescope makes faraway objects look nearer. They can be used for bird-watching, stargazing … even spying on people! It's not that hard to make your own.

What you need

- Two magnifying lenses – about 2.5–3 cm (1–1.5 in) diameter (it works best if one is slightly larger than the other)
- A cardboard tube – paper towel roll or wrapping paper roll
- Masking tape
- A pair of scissors
- A tape measure
- A newspaper or magazine
- A friend

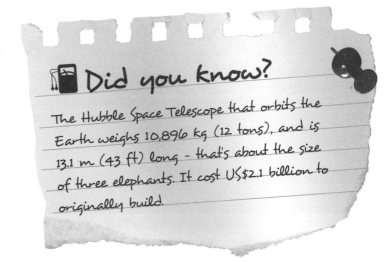

Did you know?

The Hubble Space Telescope that orbits the Earth weighs 10,896 kg (12 tons), and is 13.1 m (43 ft) long – that's about the size of three elephants. It cost US$2.1 billion to originally build.

What you do

1 | Hold the larger lens between you and the newspaper. The image of the print will look blurry.

2 | Hold the smaller lens between your eye and the first lens.

3 | Move the second lens forward or backward until the print comes into sharp focus. You will notice that the print appears larger and upside down.

4 | Hold still and get your friend to measure the distance between the two magnifying lenses and write down the distance.

5 | Cut a slot in the cardboard, about 2.5 cm (1 in) away from the front opening. Do not cut all the way through the tube. The slot should be able to hold the large lens.

6 | Cut a second slot in the tube the same distance from the first slot as your friend wrote down. This is where the smaller lens will go.

7 | Place the lenses into their slots (larger one at front, smaller one at back) and tape them into place.

8 | Leave about 1–2 cm (0.5–1 in) of tube behind the small lens and cut off any excess tube.

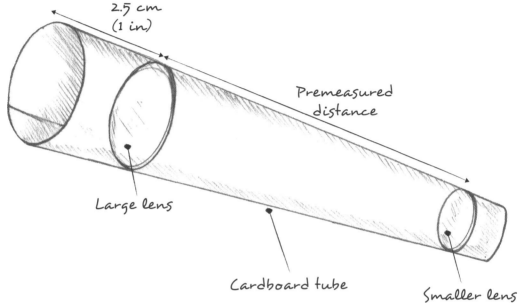

2.5 cm
(1 in)

Premeasured
distance

Large lens

Cardboard tube

Smaller lens

9 | Point your telescope at something and look through it. You should be able to look at the moon and some star clusters as well as terrestrial objects (like birds).

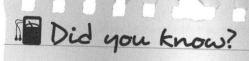 Did you know?

The word "telescope" comes from the Greek words tele, meaning "far," and skopein meaning "to look or see." Put the two words together and you get teleskopos, which means "far-seeing."

Did you know?

The first working telescope was made in 1608 by Hans Lippershey, a lens maker from Middelburg in the Netherlands.

Blast off with your own rocket

Have you ever dreamed of being an astronaut and launching into space aboard a rocket? It takes many years of study and training to become an astronaut. But, in the meantime, you can make and launch your very own rocket in your backyard.

What you need

- A sheet of A4 paper
- A plastic 35 mm film canister (one with a cap that fits INSIDE the rim instead of over the outside of the rim)
- Sticky tape
- Scissors
- Water
- Fizzing antacid tablet (the kind used to settle an upset stomach)
- Eye protection (like sunglasses or safety glasses)

What you do

1   Photocopy and enlarge the rocket template so it fits an A4 piece of paper. Cut out the template pieces.

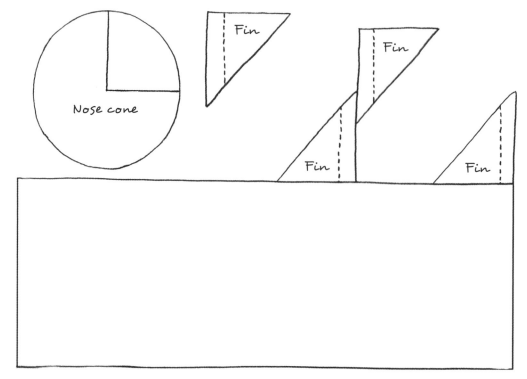

2 | Take the lid off the film canister. Use some sticky tape to stick the large rectangle of paper you cut from the template to the canister. Make sure the open end of the canister is right at the edge of the paper.

3 | Now roll the paper around the canister to form a cylinder and fasten it with sticky tape. The canister should be at the bottom of the cylinder.

4 | Take the nose cone template. Use sticky tape to fasten the ends together to form a cone shape. Stick the cone onto the top of the paper cylinder.

5 | Take the fin templates and fold along the dotted lines. Stick them to the base of the rocket. Your rocket is now ready to launch!

6 | Take your rocket outside and put on a pair of glasses to protect your eyes.

7 | Turn the rocket upside down and fill half the canister with water.

8 | Drop half of an antacid tablet into the canister and quickly put the lid back on.

9 | Stand your rocket on a launch platform, such as your footpath or driveway. Stand back and wait. In a few seconds, your rocket will blast off!

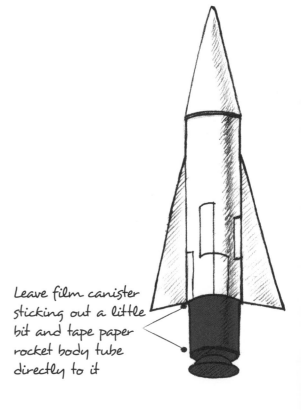

Leave film canister sticking out a little bit and tape paper rocket body tube directly to it

How it works

The tablet starts to fizz when it is put inside the canister of water. With the lid on, the fizz creates lots of gas inside but it cannot get out. Eventually, something has to give! So the canister pops its lid. All the water and gas rush down and out, pushing the canister up, along with the rocket attached to it.

Real rockets work in a similar way. Instead of water and an antacid tablet, different types of fuel are mixed inside the rocket's tank, causing an explosion. The explosion pushes out from the bottom of the tank, causing the rocket to launch upward.

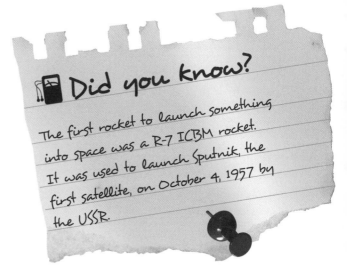

Did you know?

The first rocket to launch something into space was a R-7 ICBM rocket. It was used to launch Sputnik, the first satellite, on October 4, 1957 by the USSR.

Construct the ultimate suctioning bug catcher

Have you ever tried to catch insects in a bug catcher? It can sometimes be a little difficult enticing the little critters into the catcher.

Well, now you can suck them into your very own homemade bug catcher.

What you need

- A craft knife
- A clear disposable drink cup with a lid (the sort of cup that has a hole in the lid for a large straw)
- Clear sticky tape
- A small square of gauze

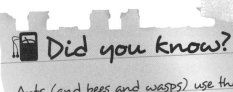

- A drinking straw
- A low-temperature glue gun
- Aquarium tubing, 1.5 cm (0.5 in) wide and 30 cm (1 ft) long

What you do

1 | Cut off a 5 cm (2 in) piece of drinking straw.

2 | Tape the gauze securely over one end of the straw.

3 | Use the craft knife to make a small straw-size opening in the bottom of the cup.

4 | Poke the straw through the hole. Seal the straw in place with the glue gun.

5 | Push one end of the aquarium tubing about 2.5 cm (1 in) through the opening in the cup's lid and seal it in place with the glue gun.

📓 Did you know?

Ants (and bees and wasps) use their antennae to taste their food before they eat it.

📓 Did you know?

A female housefly can lay between 500 and 600 eggs during her life.

6 | When the glue has dried, place the lid on the cup. To use the bug catcher, just place the free end of the tube near an unsuspecting insect and suck through the straw. The bug will zip into the viewing chamber (the gauze over the straw prevents any swallowing incidents), where you can examine it before popping off the lid to set it free.

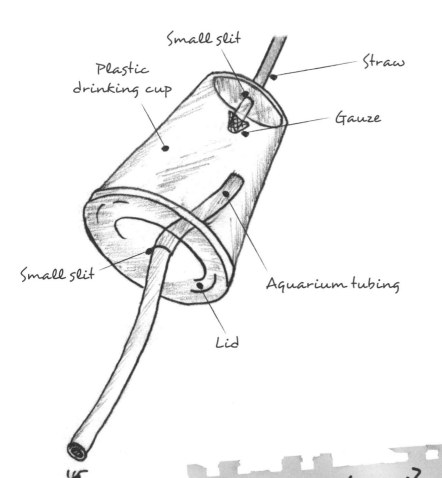

Small slit

Plastic drinking cup

Straw

Gauze

Small slit

Aquarium tubing

Lid

Did you know?

Australia has over 200 species of mosquito.

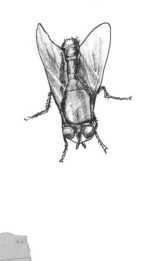

Did you know?

Crickets and grasshoppers have their ears on their front legs.

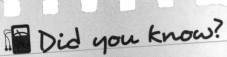

Did you know?

Cockroaches have been around for about 280 million years. They can grow back their appendages (wings, limbs, and antennae), and have been known to survive for extended periods of time without their heads!

Warning!

Don't try to suck up any bugs that are bigger than the straw, or it could get messy!

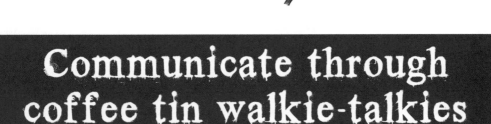

Communicate through coffee tin walkie-talkies

You all know about using plastic cups and string to make simple walkie-talkies. Well, it works a lot better with metal than with plastic.

What you need

- Metal coffee tins
- Hammer and nail
- Two screws
- A length of wire
- A friend to talk to

Did you know?

The original walkie-talkie referred to a back-mounted model, while the handheld version was called handie-talkie.

The proper name for a walkie-talkie is a handheld transceiver.

What you do

1 | Use a hammer and nail to put a small hole in the bottom of each coffee tin.

2 | Screw the screws into the holes.

3 | Tie one end of the wire to one screw and the other end to the other screw.

4 | You and your friend each take a coffee tin and go into different rooms. Make sure the wire is pulled tight.

5 | Talk to each other!

Variations

Try different lengths of wire and see if that makes a difference to the sound. How long a piece of wire can you use? Try different wire thicknesses.

Did you know?

A real walkie-talkie is a handheld, portable, two-way radio transceiver. Canadian inventor Donald Lewis Hings developed the first one, which he called a packset, in 1937. It was further refined for the Canadian government during the Second World War. After the war, the use of walkie-talkies spread to include monitoring public safety and eventually to commercial work. Nowadays you can buy walkie-talkies as toys.

The first radio receiver/transmitter to be nicknamed "Walkie-Talkie" was the backpacked Motorola SCR-300, created by an engineering team in 1940 at the Galvin Manufacturing Company.

Keep time on a lemon-powered clock

What's the ultimate in green living? A citrus-powered household! A completely lemon-powered home may not be practical, but how about a lemon-powered clock?

Remember the potato battery we made on page 91? Well, this is pretty much the same thing – except we're using lemons instead of potatoes, and a clock instead of LED.

What you need

- Three fresh lemons
- Three 5 cm (2 in) long pieces of single-strand copper wire
- Three 5 cm (2 in) galvanized nails
- Four alligator clip leads (two with clips on both ends of the lead; two with clips on one end and a wire at the other)

- A small battery-powered LCD clock
- Sandpaper or steel wool
- Electrical tape

Did you know?

A device for measuring time without making a sound was called a "timepiece."

What you do

1	Scuff the nail and copper wire with the sandpaper or steel wool until they are shiny.
2	Push a nail and a piece of wire into the flat side of a lemon about 2.5 cm (1 in). Make sure they don't touch – keep them 2.5 cm (1 in) or more apart. Repeat this step with the second and third lemon. Let's call the lemons A, B, and C.
3	Use a single-sided alligator clip lead to connect the copper wire of lemon A (with the clip) to the positive (+) connection of the digital clock (tape the bare wire to the terminal).
4	Use a single-sided alligator clip lead to connect the galvanized nail of lemon C (with the clip) to the negative (−) connection of the digital clock (tape the bare wire to the terminal).
5	Use a double-sided alligator clip lead to connect the galvanized nail of lemon A to the copper wire of lemon B.

6 | Use a double-sided alligator clip lead to connect the galvanized nail of lemon B to the copper wire of lemon C.

7 | That's it! As you connect the final lead, your digital clock should spring into life.

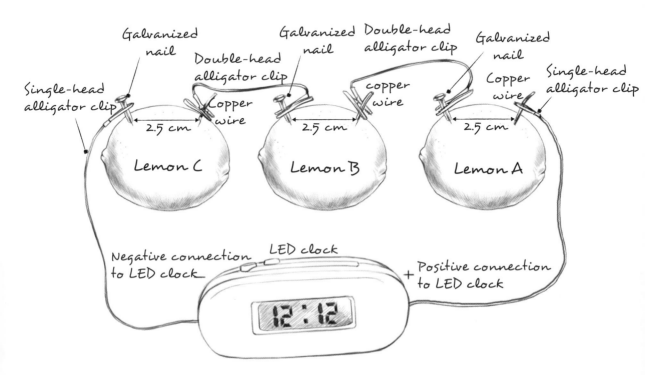

Did you know?

Horology is the art or science of measuring time.

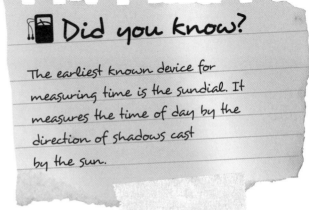

Did you know?

The earliest known device for measuring time is the sundial. It measures the time of day by the direction of shadows cast by the sun.

Did you know?

A chronometer is a timepiece with a special mechanism for ensuring and adjusting its accuracy. Chronometers are used in scientific experiments, navigation, and astronomical observations, where accuracy is extremely important.

Did you know?

Today, a "clock" refers to any device for measuring and displaying the time, which is not worn on the person - if it's being worn, then it's a watch. The word "clock" is derived from the Celtic words clagan and clocca meaning "bell." So the term "clock" originally meant a device that announced intervals of time by ringing a bell, a set of chimes, or making some kind of sound.

Capture the moment with a pinhole camera

Photographic cameras are really complex pieces of equipment, aren't they? But they are based on a very simple process of light coming through a hole and exposing a piece of film. The process is so simple that you can build a working camera out of a box.

What you need

- A box or tin with a tight-fitting lid – It should be about 8–15 cm (3–6 in) deep. It can be round or square, but a square box will be easier to keep still when taking a photo.

- Matte black paint (do not use gloss)

- A no. 10 sewing needle

- Black paper

- Masking tape or sticky tape

- Scissors

- Film – You can use a roll of black-and-white 120 size film or sheet film. Sheet film is more expensive but it is easier to use because it is flat. (You can get the film from a photographic supply store.)

What you do

1 | Paint the inside of the box with black paint. This will be the body of your camera, and the paint will prevent light reflections when taking a photo.

2 | Push a no. 10 sewing needle through the bottom of the box to a point halfway up the needle. You'll get a smoother hole if you rotate the needle as you push it through. A no. 10 sized needle will give you the correct-sized hole. The hole should be centered in the bottom of the box.

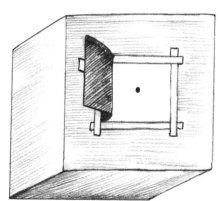

3 | Cut a piece of black paper to cover the pinhole and tape it to the outside of the box, over the hole. Tape it on the top edge only so that it can be lifted like a flap. You can use a second smaller piece of tape to hold down the flap until you are ready to take your photo.

4 | Now here comes the tricky bit. You need to load your camera in the dark – a closet in a darkened room should do. If you are using sheet film, simply cut a square to fit into the lid of your camera and tape it into place, shiny side up. If you are using a roll of film, you will need to unroll it and cut a square. It will be harder to tape down because it is curved. After the film is taped into place, tightly close the lid of the camera.

Did you know?

The first permanent photograph was an image produced in 1826 by the French inventor Nicéphore Niépce. The picture took eight hours to expose.

5   Now you are ready to take a photo. Go outdoors – you'll get better light this way. Position your camera, making sure the flap (with the pinhole behind it) is pointing at what you want to photograph. Make sure the camera is on a steady surface, like a table, and put a weight on it (a book will do) to stop it from moving around.

6   Lift the flap to take the photo. How long you need to hold the flap open will depend on the speed of your film and how bright it is when you're taking the photo. If you are using 100 speed film, you will need about two to four seconds on a sunny day, but about eight to 16 seconds on a cloudy day. If you are using 400 speed film, you will need about one or two seconds on a sunny day, but about four to eight seconds on a cloudy day. You will probably need to experiment a little before you get it right. Don't forget, you have to take your film out in complete darkness as well, and keep it in darkness until it is developed.

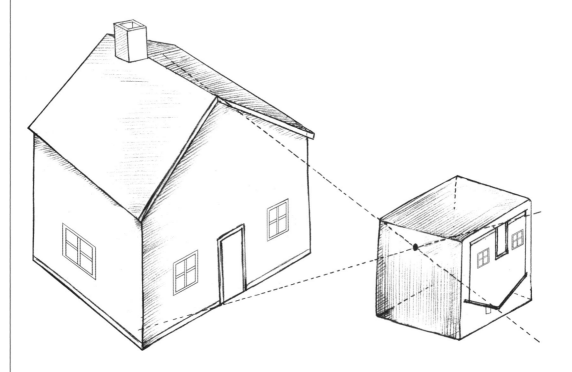

7   As with an ordinary camera, taking a photo with your pinhole camera will create a negative image. You will need to develop the negative and print a picture from it. You can take it to a photographic store (you'll probably need to take it to a specialist store rather than a one-hour photo shop), or you could set up your own darkroom and learn how to develop and print your own photos. There are lots of books available on the subject.

How it works

Objects reflect light. Different colored objects reflect different amounts of light. The pinhole focuses the light reflected by objects, onto the film, which is coated with chemicals that make an image of the light being reflected.

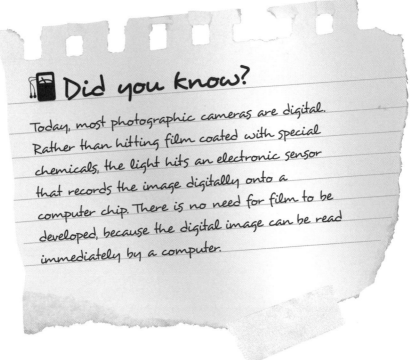

Did you know?

Today, most photographic cameras are digital. Rather than hitting film coated with special chemicals, the light hits an electronic sensor that records the image digitally onto a computer chip. There is no need for film to be developed, because the digital image can be read immediately by a computer.

Make an animated movie wheel

Animation is a trick! Your eyes are tricked into seeing a series of still progressive images as a moving image. Want to trick your own eyes? You can, by making an animated movie wheel.

What you need

- A piece of thin cardboard at least 18 cm (7 in) square
- Glue
- Scissors

- Two small coins
- A black marker (or paint)
- A nail
- A bathroom mirror

What you do

1 | Photocopy the template.

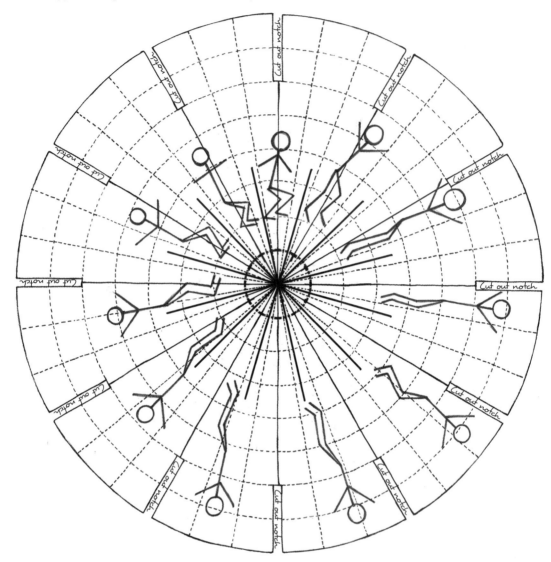

2 | Glue the template onto the cardboard.

3 | Cut out the circle, and then the notches.

4 | Turn it over and use the black marker (or black paint) to color in the areas between the notches, all the way around the circle.

5 | Use the sticky tape to attach the two coins to the back of the wheel as shown in the diagram. The coins will weight the wheel and make it spin longer.

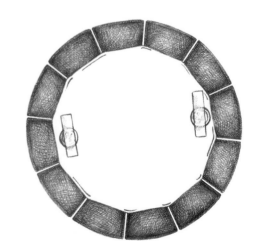

6 | Push the nail through the center of the wheel and put some tape over the pointy end so you don't hurt yourself.

7 | Hold your wheel by the nail, in front of a mirror with the printed side facing the mirror. Look at the reflection through the notches and spin the wheel. Watch the picture move.

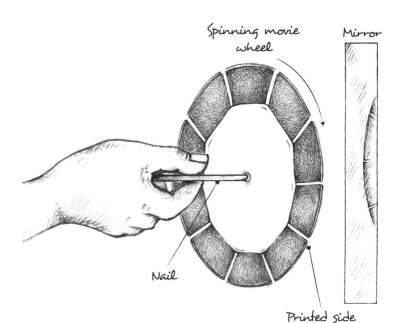

Spinning movie wheel

Mirror

Nail

Printed side to mirror

What next?

Look carefully at the pictures on the template. See how they are progressive. Use the template to create another wheel, but this time, use sticky tape to attach the template to the cardboard. Then, when you've cut it out, detach the template and draw your own pictures onto the cardboard.

Did you know?

The earliest known animation is a 5,200-year-old earthen bowl found in Iran. It has five images painted along the sides. When the bowl is spun, it shows a goat leaping up to a tree to take a pear.

Did you know?

Many people think that Disney's Snow White and the Seven Dwarfs (1937) was the first animated feature film. This is not true. The world's first animated feature film was actually made 20 years earlier in 1917 by Argentinian cartoonist Quirino Cristiani. It is a silent, black-and-white film called El Apóstol.

Did you know?

"Animation" means "brought to life."

Did you know?

An animated movie wheel, like the one you have made, is called a phenakistoscope.

Catch an intruder with a homemade alarm

Want to know if someone is entering your house? Want to keep your pesky brother or sister out of your room? You could set an alarm to go off if someone steps into a room. Where do you get an alarm like this? You make it!

What you need

- Sticky tape
- A 9-volt battery
- A mini buzzer
- About 20 paper clips
- Kitchen foil – about 30 cm (1 ft)
- A length of insulated wire
- Drinking straws
- A lightweight mat

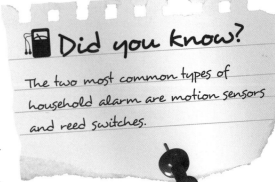

Did you know?

The two most common types of household alarm are motion sensors and reed switches.

What you do

1 | Fold the foil to a size of about 15 cm × 20 cm (6 in × 8 in).

2 | Strip the ends of the wire so that you have bare wire. Attach one end to the negative (−) terminal of the battery. Sticky tape the other end onto the foil (make sure that the bare wire is in contact with the foil).

3 | Connect the negative (−) wire of the mini buzzer to a paper clip. Then connect the remaining paper clips to form a paper clip chain.

4 | Connect the positive (+) wire of the mini buzzer to the positive (+) terminal of the battery.

5 | Touch the paper clip chain to the foil. This will complete the electrical circuit and the buzzer should sound. Now it's time to set the alarm.

6 | Choose a location – for example, just inside your front door.

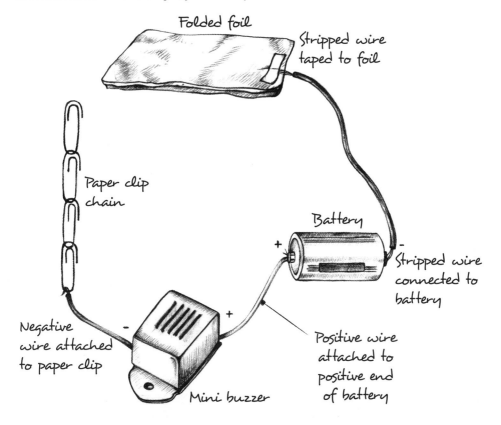

Folded foil

Stripped wire taped to foil

Paper clip chain

Battery

Stripped wire connected to battery

Negative wire attached to paper clip

Positive wire attached to positive end of battery

Mini buzzer

7 | Lie the paper clip chain flat, down in front of the door. Place the straws about 2.5 cm (1 in) to either side of the chain, parallel with the chain. Use the sticky tape to secure the chain and straws.

8 | Conceal the buzzer to the side of the door.

9 | Lie the foil on top of the straws so it doesn't touch the paper clips.

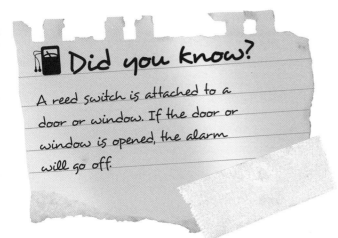

Did you know?

A reed switch is attached to a door or window. If the door or window is opened, the alarm will go off.

Did you know?

A motion sensor detects movement. A person stepping into a room with a motion sensor will set off the alarm.

10 | Carefully put a lightweight mat over the chain, straws, and foil. Your alarm is now set.

11 | When someone enters, they will step on the mat – the straws will squash, allowing the foil to touch the paper clip chain, completing the electrical circuit and setting off the buzzer.

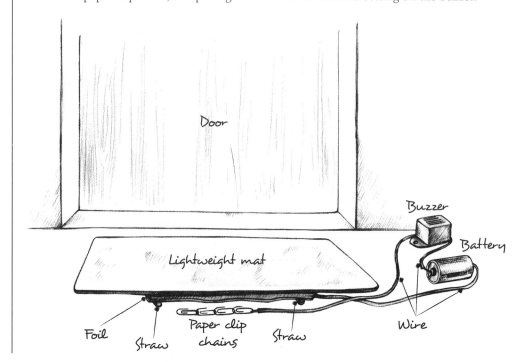

Build a radio

There are all sorts of radios: big radios that are part of a larger system, car radios, and portable radios with headphones. This is a really simple radio that you can build yourself.

What you need

- A wooden board, about 15 cm × 20 cm (6 in × 8 in)

- A toilet paper roll

- A spool of magnet wire

- A spool of insulated wire (when attaching pieces of wire, make sure to remove the insulation from the ends so you have bare wire to make the connection)

- A pair of earphones

- Four metal drawing pins

- Three nails

- A used blade from a safety razor – If you can get a blue razor blade, which has been heated, it will work better. If not, get a used one, preferably rusty.

- A big safety pin

- A pencil with a fat lead

What you do

1 | Poke a hole at each end of the toilet roll. Thread one end of the magnet wire through one hole and tie it off, leaving about 7.5 cm (3 in) loose. Carefully wind the wire around the roll. Do this until you have a total of 120 turns of wire around the roll. Make sure the turns lie side by side, not one on top of the other. Tie the wire off in the second hole, leave about 7.5 cm (3 in), and cut off any excess. This is your radio's coil.

2 | Lay the coil on its side on the board, close to one end. Use two of the drawing pins to fasten it to the board. Make sure the drawing pins do not touch any part of the wire.

3 | Hammer a nail into the board on either side of the coil – about 4 cm (1.5 in) from the roll.

4 | Attach the wires from either end of the coil to the nails.

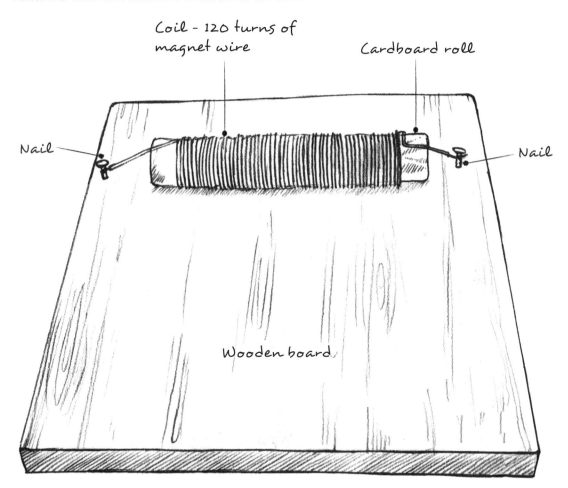

Coil - 120 turns of magnet wire

Cardboard roll

Nail

Nail

Wooden board

5 | Put the razor blade in place at the opposite end of the board to the coil. Be very careful when you handle the blade – it is VERY sharp. Lay the blade flat on the board and fix it in place with two drawing pins. Do not push the pins all the way into the board.

6 | Sharpen the pencil so that you have a long piece of lead showing. Break off the lead and put it next to the point of the safety pin. Use a piece of wire to attach the piece of lead to the point of the safety pin. Use the pliers to bend the head of the pin back so that it lies flat on the board.

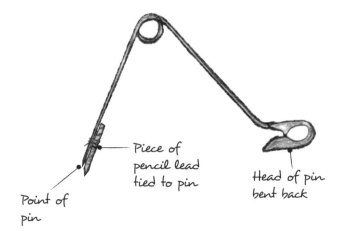

Piece of
pencil lead
tied to pin

Head of pin
bent back

Point of
pin

7 | Place the safety pin to the right of the razor blade so that the lead point rests on the razor blade. Put one of the nails through the head of the pin and, with the hammer, drive the nail into the board until it almost touches the pin.

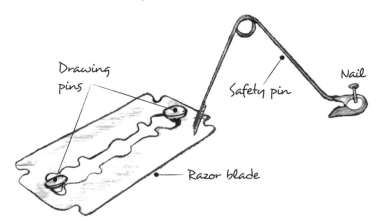

Drawing
pins

Nail

Safety pin

Razor blade

8 | Attach a wire to the left-hand drawing pin on the razor blade Push the pin down as hard as you can so that the bare wire is against the blade. Then take the other end of this wire and wrap it around the nail to the left of the coil.

9 | Attach a wire to the nail to the right of the coil. Take the other end of this wire and wrap it around one of the metal tips on the cord of the earphones.

10 | Attach another wire to the other metal tip of the earphone cord. Now take the other end of this wire and put it under the head of the nail that holds the safety pin. Hammer in the nail so that the pin will stand up. Don't nail it too tightly, as the pin needs to be able to move a little.

11 | Attach another wire to the nail that connects with the coil and razor blade. This will be the aerial. The longer the aerial, the better. Let it dangle out of a window. Or, better yet, perhaps you can get a long length of wire and string it from a window out to a tree.

12 | Attach another piece of wire to the nail connecting the coil to the earphones. This will be your grounding wire. You need to connect it to something that goes into the ground. The best ground connection is a cold water pipe. Wind the bare end of the wire around a pipe that only has cold water running through it.

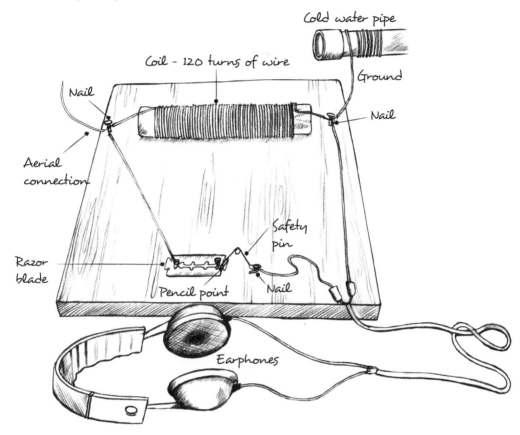

Cold water pipe

Coil – 120 turns of wire

Ground

Nail

Nail

Aerial connection

Safety pin

Razor blade

Pencil point

Nail

Earphones

13 | Put on the earphones, and do not make any noise in the room where you have your set. With your finger, move the pin very gently so that the little piece of lead goes across the razor blade. You should start to hear very faint little crackling noises in your earphones. Continue to move the pin until you find a station. Move the pin very slowly and listen very carefully. You will only be able to pick up the stations that are closest to you and they may only be faint.

What next?

Do you want to improve your radio and get better reception? You can, by buying a crystal detector from an electronics store and attaching it in place of the razor blade and safety pin setup. It works in a similar way – a piece of crystal taking the place of the razor blade.

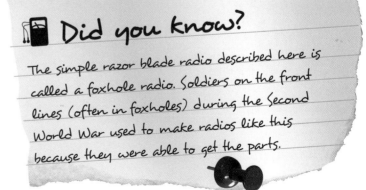

Did you know?

The simple razor blade radio described here is called a foxhole radio. Soldiers on the front lines (often in foxholes) during the Second World War used to make radios like this because they were able to get the parts.

TRICKERY

Learn some no-fail card tricks

Most card tricks, while blowing the minds of observers, usually have a fairly simple trick at their core. Here are a couple of classic card tricks that will baffle your rivals and win favor of people you want to impress.

The "who's lying" card trick

What you need

- A deck of cards
- A table

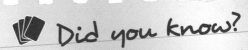

Did you know?

Don't repeat tricks, even if your audience begs you to. It is far more likely that your trick will be uncovered if people observe it more than once.

What you do

1 | Shuffle the deck of cards before your audience arrives. Make sure you know which card is on the bottom.

2 | Once your audience is seated, fan out the deck of cards facedown on the table and ask a volunteer to choose one card. They are not to show or tell you its identity.

3 | While the volunteer looks at the card, you should close the fan of cards, straighten the deck, and place it on the table, facedown. Ask the volunteer to cut the deck into two equal piles. Now ask your volunteer to put their card on the pile they cut from the top of the deck.

4 | Place the other half of the deck on top of the volunteer's card. This should mean the card you memorized, which was at the bottom of the pile a minute ago, is now on top of the selected card.

5 | Now is the time for some good magician's patter. Explain to the audience the deck of cards is special – it can detect lies.

6 | Explain to your volunteer that you are going to turn each card over and ask them if this is the card they selected. They are to say "no" every time, even when you turn over the selected card. The deck of cards will "tell" you when the volunteer is lying. Obviously, you are looking for the card you memorized – the card after it will be the selected card.

7 | When you turn over the selected card and your volunteer says "No," yell "Liar!" loudly and watch the reaction.

Listen to "talking cards"

What you need

- A deck of cards with no jokers
- A table

What you do

1 | Explain to your audience that you have special powers, which enable you to hear "talking" cards.

2 | Ask a volunteer to deal out the cards faceup on the table. They must deal them out in a single row until you say stop. You should mentally count the number of cards being dealt, taking note of the seventh card. When your volunteer reaches 26, tell them to stop and say something like, "That should be enough."

3 | Tell the audience you'll select a card at random – pretend to consider the cards, and then point to the seventh card. Ask your volunteer to tell the audience the name of the selected card. Explain that you will be able to find the card again with the help of your "talking" cards.

4 | Pick up the cards, ensuring the seventh one stays in the seventh position. Put the cards facedown on the table in a pile and put the rest of the deck on top. Slowly deal out the cards so that they lie faceup in a column. Tell the audience the cards are "talking" to you. Note the number of the first card. Continue to deal and silently count from that number until you reach 10. For example, if the first card is a 4, the next card becomes 5, then 6, 7, 8, 9, and 10 – no matter what the numbers on the cards actually are.

5 | Once you reach the number 10, start another column – all the while pretending the cards are "talking" to you. If the first card you turn over in a column is a 10 or a face card, it counts as 10 and so you must begin the next column. Aces count as 1.

6 | Make three columns and then stop. While pretending you are listening, you should be adding up the first cards on the table from each column, perhaps a 10, 3, and 2, which would make 15. This number is the key to finding the selected card!

7 | Now tell the audience the cards have told you the location of the selected card. Tell the volunteer to deal off the same number of cards as your total – in our example, 15. The fifteenth card will be your selected card! Everyone will be amazed.

Pull a specific card from the deck

What you need

- A deck of cards

What you do

1 Ask a volunteer to shuffle the deck of cards.

2 When the deck is handed back to you, straighten it, taking note of which card is facedown on top. Perhaps it is the ten of diamonds.

3 Hold the deck vertically in one hand (left if you are right-handed and right if you are left-handed), so the cards are facing the audience.

4 Place your other hand behind the deck and rest your forefinger or index finger on top of the deck. Now extend your little finger (or ring finger if it is easier) until it touches the back of the top card (the ten of diamonds).

Push on and upward with this finger

5 Now all you need to do is name the card and ask it to rise for you! "Ten of diamonds … arise now from your slumber!" While you say, push upward on the top card with your little or ring finger. Do it slowly, making sure your forefinger or index finger is rising as you speak. From where the audience is sitting it will look as if your forefinger or index finger is encouraging the rising card to rise, and it will also look as if the card is coming from the middle of the deck. Easy but effective!

Use mathematics to astonish with cards

In this trick, you ask a volunteer to deal you a card seemingly at random – but in fact, you already know the card's identity!

What you need

- A deck of cards

- A table

What you do

1 | Before your show, memorize the tenth card from the top of a deck of cards.

2 | Begin the trick by giving a volunteer the pack of cards. Ask them to think of a number between 10 and 20, and then ask them to deal that number of cards facedown into a pile on the table. The rest of the deck can be put aside.

3 | Now your volunteer needs to add together the two digits that make up the number they selected. If they selected the number 14, for example, they would add 1 and 4 to get 5. They then deal that number of cards, 5, from the pile and look at the fifth card without telling anyone what it is. This card will be the card you memorized before the trick – the original tenth card.

4 | Pretend to read the volunteer's mind – perhaps you'd like to heighten the drama by drawing the card on a piece of paper, or you could ask the volunteer to return the card to the deck and shuffle the cards. They hand the deck to you and you "select" the card by "reading" the fingerprints!

Master some coin tricks

The good thing about coin tricks is that you can perform them just about anywhere and your props can be easily obtained (check behind the couch). You don't need a lengthy setup or patter, so, with a bit of practice, you will be able to bring a quick bit of mischief to everyday situations.

Learn sleight of hand

All magicians learn sleight of hand. Learn this trick well and you can perform it at any time in any place.

What you need

- A coin

What you do

1   Begin by placing the coin firmly between the index and middle fingers of one hand. The coin should be hidden so that when you present your open hand (palm out) to the audience they can't see a thing.

2   Now we come to the part that you need to practice and practice. To produce the coin you turn your fingers in toward the palm of your hand and use your thumb to bring the coin to the front.

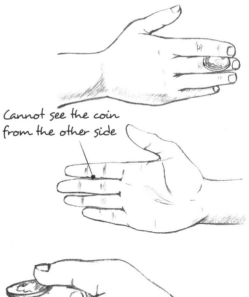

Cannot see the coin from the other side

Coin snatch

The idea is to put a coin in the palm of your hand and challenge a volunteer to snatch it from your hand. Your volunteer can't do it, but when you switch places, you get the coin on your first try.

What you need

• A coin

What you do

1   Gather your audience and put the coin on your palm and keep it flat. Ask a volunteer to grab the coin before you close your hand – be as quick as you can. Your volunteer will fail every time.

2   Now swap. Your volunteer must hold the coin in exactly the same way as you did – flat on the palm of their hand.

3   How do you do it? Ok, place your fingers and thumb together, without touching, and make sure these fingers are pointing down toward the coin.

4   Quickly move your hand down, gently striking the palm of your volunteer's hand with your fingertips. This action means the volunteer's hand will be pushed downward a little and the coin will jump up into your waiting fingers! Try it! It works!

The coin fold

Another easy but effective trick using just one coin – especially suitable for a small audience.

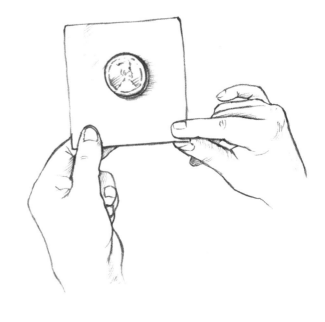

What you need

- A coin
- A small piece of paper

What you do

1	Place the coin in the center of the piece of paper.
2	Fold the bottom edge of the paper up and over the coin, leaving a 6 mm (0.25 in) gap between the two edges of the paper.
3	Fold the right edge of the paper back behind the coin.
4	Fold the left edge of the paper back behind the coin.

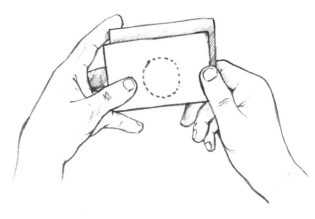

5 | Make the final fold by bending the top flap of the paper back behind the coin. It seems as if the coin is completely wrapped, but in fact the top edge is still open.

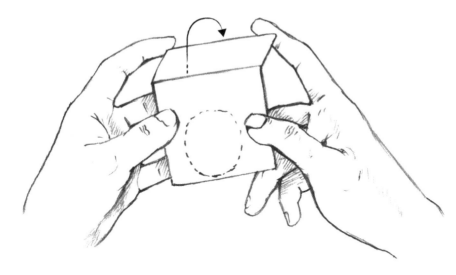

6 | You now turn the package around so the open edge allows the coin to slip into the palm of your hand, where it stays while you "prove" the coin has disappeared by tearing up the paper package.

The master of illusion

Although you need many coins for this trick, you actually use none! Your audience will think you are throwing a coin from hand to hand, but it's all an illusion!

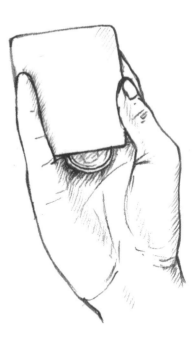

What you need

• A pocketful of change

What you do

1 | Make a show of taking a handful of coins from your pocket – let the audience see the coins are real. Choose one coin and pretend to pick it up – you'll need to practice this! Return the coins to your pocket.

2   Throw the imaginary coin back and forth from one hand to the other,
    making a small slapping sound as you pretend to catch the coin each time.
    Practice with a real coin so you can get the sound right, but if you loosen
    your fingers and slap the heel of your palm as you "catch" your coin, it
    should sound OK.

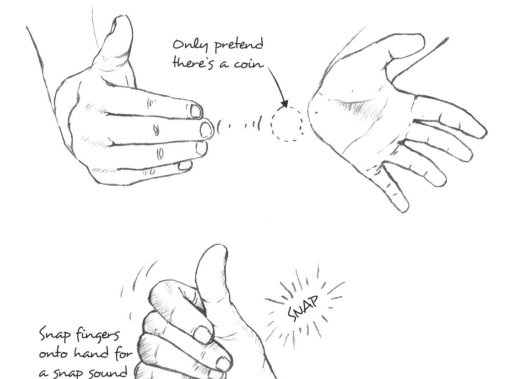

Only pretend
there's a coin

Snap fingers
onto hand for
a snap sound
(like a coin
hitting!)

SNAP

3   Do this several times, and then stop and pretend
    to hold the imaginary coin in one hand. Ask your
    audience to guess how it landed – "Heads or tails?."
    Of course, upon opening your hand there is no
    coin. That's okay because the audience assumes it's
    now in your other hand.

4   Slowly open your other hand to reveal
    no coin there either – and bow while your
    audience applauds.

Master the old three cup trick

This is one of the oldest and most famous magic tricks. It requires some props, but if you are serious about being a trickster, you absolutely need to have the old three cup trick up your sleeve.

What you need

- Three cups
- Four small sponge balls
- One larger sponge ball

Tip

The special cups used in this trick can be purchased wherever magic props are sold. Consider buying a set of clear plastic cups to begin with so you can see exactly where each ball is as you learn.

Each cup has a rim, which prevents another cup being pushed completely inside it, enabling a ball to be hidden in the space created. Also, the bottom of each cup has an indent, which allows a soft sponge ball to rest without rolling off.

What you do

1 | To prepare, place the large ball in your left pocket and one small ball in each of the three cups, and the fourth small ball in your left hand. The cups are then placed inside each other. They should be sitting mouth-up.

2 | When you begin the performance, turn each cup over quickly, keeping the ball hidden underneath.

3 | Tap or wave your hand over all the cups and then lift the right-hand one (with your right hand) showing a ball resting on the table underneath it. Transfer the cup to your left hand so it covers the small ball hidden there.

4 | Repeat with the other two cups, showing the two other balls and sitting the cups on top of the one already in your left hand.

5 | Now place each cup mouth-down directly behind each ball on the table. Place one first to the right and then the left so the first cup now becomes the central cup. As you place this cup on the table, make sure the concealed ball drops into it as you turn it upside down.

6 | Pick up one of the balls and place it on top of the central cup. Next, place both the other cups on top and, with a tap or wave of your hand, lift all three cups as one to reveal a ball on the table. To the audience it appears as though you have magically made the ball pass through the base of the cup. Wait for the applause ... and then say: "But wait! There's more!"

7 | Again, separate the cups and place them mouth-down on the table, this time putting the cup that contains the extra ball in the middle over the ball already on the table. Place a ball on top of this cup and repeat step 6. The difference could be that you invite an audience member to tap the cup – while your volunteer is doing this, you take the large ball from your pocket, holding it in your left hand.

8 | Again, lift all three cups as one and, astonishingly, all three small balls are on the table. Casually place the cups over your left hand and act as though the trick is finished by placing all three cups (and the larger ball) on the table.

9 | A bit of acting here will earn you enormous applause, so hesitate as if you want to tell your audience something, but shouldn't. Then say you'll reveal a magic secret – you did use more than three balls for the trick! Pick up the cups to reveal a much larger ball – to more applause!

Perform magic with your handkerchief

Another classic, this trick uses a silky hankie – a classic magician's prop. You can do this trick practically anywhere.

What you need

- A small rubber band
- A large patterned silk handkerchief
- A ring
- A table

What you do

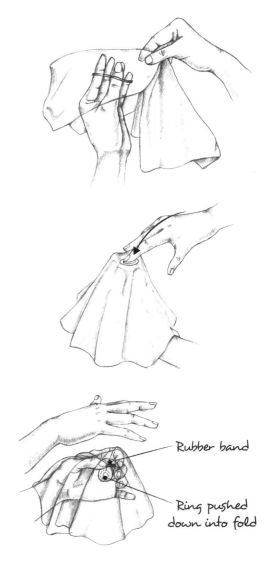

1   Before facing your audience, slip a rubber band over three of the fingers on your left hand.

2   Once your audience arrives, take out your silk hankie and wave it about using your right hand so all eyes are on it and not on the rubber band over your fingers. (You don't want your audience to notice the rubber band.)

3   Spread the hankie over your left hand with a flourish and secretly slip your thumb into the rubber band to widen it a little more.

4   Ask your audience if you can borrow a ring (of course, if they haven't got one, you will use your own ring, which you happen to have brought with you!)

5   Show everyone the ring and then place it on the silk hankie above the rubber band. With your free hand, rub the ring saying a magic chant. Of course what you are doing is pushing the ring through the band into the fold of silk below.

6   Slip the band off your fingers to trap the ring in a fold of silk while making a dramatic gesture and saying more magic words.

Rubber band

Ring pushed down into fold

7 | Dramatically whip the hankie away with your right hand and look amazed to see that the ring has disappeared from your left hand.

8 | Return the ring by spreading the silk over your left hand again, reach into the folds with your right hand, and pull out the ring with a smile!

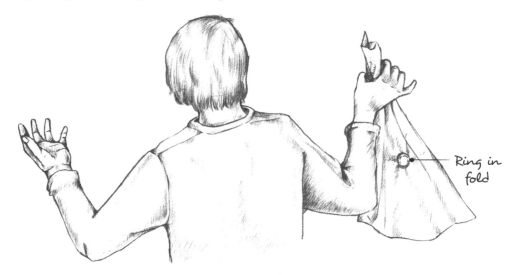

Ring in fold

Slice a banana without peeling it

Your unsuspecting victim grabs a banana from the fruit bowl to enjoy a little snack. They snap open the peel at the top and begin to peel the banana. They can't believe what they see inside. The banana has been cut into slices, all the way down. It looks ready to go into a fruit salad. They have no idea how it happened, and you may want to keep silent on this one, to keep them baffled.

What you need

- A banana with a firm skin

- A thin, long needle

What you do

1 | Take a needle and poke it through the banana skin, near the top. Be careful, the needle doesn't come out the other side.

2 | Wiggle the needle from side to side (without making the hole any bigger) until you have cut a slice inside the banana.

3 | Now take the needle out and make another hole, a little way down. Again, insert the needle and slice.

4 | Do this all the way down the banana.

5 | When you have finished, put the banana at the top of the fruit bowl and wait for your victim to come along.

6 | Watch their face as they unpeel the banana and discover that it has already been sliced for them!

Variation

If your victim is particularly gullible, stride up to them as they are about to peel the fruit. Tell them that you heard on the news about a new type of banana that slices itself as it grows. Explain that these bananas are harvested especially to be used in fruit salads. If the victim believes you, they may go and tell other people about the amazing new banana and you will have extra material to laugh about.

Make an apple pie bed

Also called short-sheeting, this is a classic trick, suitable to play at camps, on holiday, or when you have a guest in your home. The gist of it is this: the victim is ready for bed. They are in their pajamas, they have cleaned their teeth, and have said goodnight to everyone. They turn down the covers on their bed and put their feet under the sheet. The only problem is, they can't push their feet down to the bottom of the bed. No matter how hard they push, the sheet won't let them stretch out. The more annoyed they get, the more hilarious it will be for you, chuckling at the door. Be warned, this trick only works on beds with top sheets.

What you need

• A made bed with a top sheet. Be warned – this joke never works if you play it on a sloppy person who never makes the bed. They will suspect something immediately if they see a neatly made bed.

What you do

1 | Take the top sheet and the blanket or duvet off the bed. Hide the top sheet. You don't need it anymore.

2 | Undo the bottom sheet from the bottom end of the bed. Fold the sheet in half so that both ends are at the top end of the bed.

3 | Put the blanket or duvet back on the bed, and then fold the top part of the sheet over the top of the blanket or duvet. The sheet should now only go halfway down the bed, but from the outside, everything appears normal.

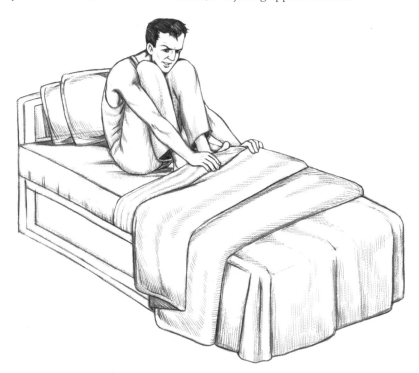

Play the great "he's deaf" prank

This is a really simple prank. In exchange for doing almost nothing at all, you are rewarded by a thigh-slappingly hilarious scene to liven up a party.

What you need

- A party full of people

- Two unsuspecting victims who don't know each other

What you do

1 | Find two perfect victims. Let's call them Bert and Morris. Let's say Bert is your best friend from kindergarten, whom you haven't seen in years. He's a bit shy and doesn't know any of your friends. Morris is a visiting cousin who also doesn't know any of your friends.

2 | Prepare the prank. All you need to do before the party is this. Call Bert and have a conversation along the following lines.

"Hello Bert, I just wanted to ask you a little favor regarding my party tomorrow. Please chat to my cousin Morris, he won't know anyone there."
Bert, being a nice guy, will reply that he is happy to do this. Then, you need to say the following lie:

"Just one word of warning, Morris is quite deaf. But don't embarrass him by bringing it up. Just speak up, for goodness sake!"

Bert is sure to agree, being a nice guy.

3 | Then, you need to call Morris and do the same thing, in reverse.

"Hello Morris, I was wondering if you could do me a favor at my party. I have an old kindergarten friend coming along. As I will be busy entertaining the guests, Bert won't have anyone to chat to. I need you to keep him company."

When Morris kindly agrees, you need to casually add: "Just speak up when you talk to him, he's a bit deaf."

4 | At the party, you can make the introduction (in a loud voice). Then you are free to walk off and you and your friends can watch the two goons bellowing at each other – for no apparent reason. It often happens that the conversation gets louder and louder, as the victims start outyelling each other. Hilarious.

Scare a friend with the "ghost" prank

This is the perfect trick to play on a gullible friend. Organize a gathering at your place. Designate an accomplice and gather a couple of people. You must brief them on the trick before the victim arrives, so invite the victim to come over after everyone else so that you can get the wheels of the trick in motion.

What you need

- An unsuspecting victim

- A gathering of people who are all in on the joke

- Special effects such as smoke, shadows, and sound effects (strange music, rattling, scratching on the walls)

What you do

1. Prepare the special effects and send your accomplice out of the room so that they can operate the special effects without the victim's knowledge.

2. When your victim arrives, welcome them and ask them to join the party. Everyone should look as if they are having a really good time – they should NOT pay the victim any special attention.

3. At some point, you or one of the guests should turn the conversation to ghosts.

4. Make sure that the victim is listening when you start talking. Remain casual while delivering the following:

   "Oh I don't believe that ghost stuff. I mean, people say this house is haunted and I've never seen anything at all! But the previous owners said that a ghost lives here."

   "Apparently, it has only appeared to certain individuals, no one else is aware of its presence. And allegedly, every person who has seen the ghost has broken out in itchy incurable hives! But I don't believe any of that stuff ..."

(You can replace hives with anything unpleasant – the person has died on the spot, lost all their hair, etc.)

5 | Now that you have the victim's attention, go back to your normal party talk.

6 | This is where your accomplice comes in. A bang is heard. No one reacts, except for your victim.

7 | When the victim says "Did anyone hear that?," you should all look at the victim and act bewildered. Hear what?

8 | This should be followed by a series of other creepy stuff, scratching on the walls, lights going on and off, and so on.

9 | Everyone at the party should act as if nothing out of the ordinary is going on, while you secretly watch your victim squirm! They may even start scratching themselves, imagining that they are breaking out in hives.

Discover the possibilities of fake blood

Fake blood is hilarious for a variety of reasons. It can alarm, scare, and disgust people. Make sure you have a great story prepared to go with your fake blood and practice acting like a person who is bleeding profusely (walking stiffly, appearing vampiric, acting as if you are about to pass out or perish). Don't do this in front of the fainthearted.

What you need

- Clear corn syrup or glucose syrup

- Red food coloring

- Water

- Sifted flour

- A tiny bit of blue food coloring

What you do

1   Add about 150 ml of corn syrup to 50 ml of water.

2   Add food coloring until the mixture is deep red. Add a drop of blue food coloring. This gives the "blood" a more realistic color. Add some more red or blue, until you are happy with the color.

3   Add a few tablespoons of flour and mix gently. Remove small lumps of flour from the top of the mixture. You have fake "blood."

4   Use a spoon or eyedropper to distribute the blood.

Variation

If you can stand the taste of corn syrup, try this variation:

1   Buy some tiny mints.

2   Store about four or five of them in your cheek, along with a teaspoon or so of fake blood (make sure you train for this – getting used to the disgusting taste of mint and corn syrup might take a while!).

3 | Join family or friends at a meal. Smile politely, and then take a bite of bread (or something else, feel free to improvise) and yell out dramatically: "This bread is stale!"

4 | With a pained expression spit into your hand, revealing lots of little tooth-like mints and fake blood.

Create homemade sneezing powder

Sneezing powder makes people sneeze uncontrollably. Seriously – what could be funnier that that?

What you need

- Some ground black pepper

- A mortar and pestle

- A small container (in the olden days, people used film canisters, but you can find any other tiny container or box)

What you do

1 | Grind the black pepper for ages, ten minutes at least. It needs to be of powdery consistency (we call it sneezing "powder" for a reason. If you want the trick to work, don't slack off).

2 | Once the pepper has been ground, put it in the small container. Make sure your container has a good lid, so that you can carry it around in your pocket, to use at particularly opportune moments.

3 | Now, sneezing powder is only effective if it goes in people's noses. So there's no point dispensing it on someone's pants or shoes because, unless they spontaneously decide to sniff their pants or shoes, they are not going to start sneezing. It is also a bad move to dispense the powder in a person's eyes. Instead of being seen as a hilarious joker, you will probably be hated and squinted at by a red-eyed victim for the rest of the day.

4 | Dispensing the powder is tricky. Don't panic; just swiftly pinch some sneezing powder at the right moment and casually throw it into the air (sneezing powder is always good in a crowd, or at a party when the lights are low).

Did you know?

If you are serious about your sneezing powder, you might also like to carry it around on a hot day, armed with one of those personal battery-operated fans. That way, you can pretend to be fanning yourself but, when the moment is right, put some sneezing powder in the palm of your hand and direct the air at your victim.

Send messages in invisible ink

Spies and secret service agents have favored the use of invisible inks to communicate with their accomplices without being discovered by the enemy. What better way to send top-secret correspondence, which will remain hidden to your enemies even if intercepted?

What you need

- A sheet of thin paper (such as tracing paper)
- Normal writing paper
- Candle wax
- A wooden skewer

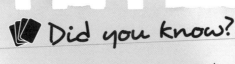

Did you know?

Some other popular inks include vinegar (developed using red cabbage water), milk, lemon juice, or white wine (developed by carefully heating the paper – the invisible ink will turn brown).

What you do

1 | Write an innocent and irrelevant message on the writing paper. This will put suspicious people off the scent.

2 | Rub the candle wax all over the thin sheet of paper until the paper is covered with a layer of wax.

3 | Put the thin paper (waxed side down) on top of your writing paper.

4 | Using the wooden skewer, press into the thin paper and write your real message on the non-waxed side. Remove the thin paper from your writing paper.

5 | The writing paper will look the same, but your secret message will be there, written in "invisible" wax.

TOP SECRET

Dear Jane,
Please find enclosed the details for your mission.
Arrive at headquarters at 12:15 am.
The password is

6 | When your accomplice receives your note, they will be able to view it by sprinkling powder (such as powdered cocoa or talcum powder) over the paper, revealing your secret message.

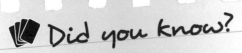

Did you know?

Carl Frederick Muller was a German spy who operated in Britain during World War I. Muller sent seemingly innocent letters (in English) to his accomplices, but used formaldehyde and lemon juice to write invisible messages in German between the lines of English text. He was eventually discovered and sentenced to death.

Win chess in less than five moves

This strategy, humiliating for your chess partner, is called "the scholar's mate." It relies on your opponent making all the right (or wrong!) moves, but you'll be surprised how often they will move exactly to your plan.

What you need

- A game of chess
- An opponent

What you do

1 | Play white so you can move first. Move your Pawn from E2 to E4.

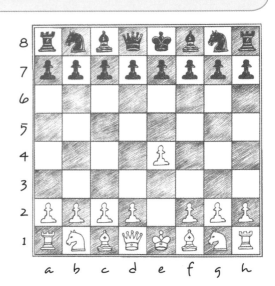

2 | Your opponent will move their Pawn, for example, from E7 to E5.

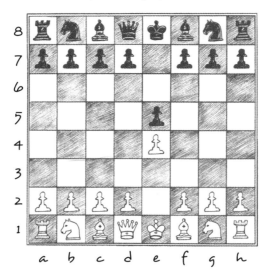

3 | Move your King's Bishop from F1 to C4.

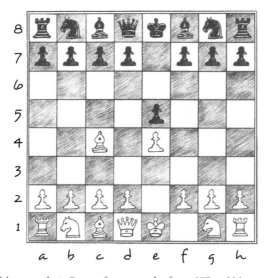

4 | Your opponent should move their Pawn, for example, from H7 to H6.

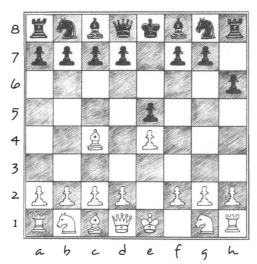

5 | Move your Queen from D1 to H5.

6 | Your opponent moves their King's Knight from G8 to F6, hoping to take your Queen.

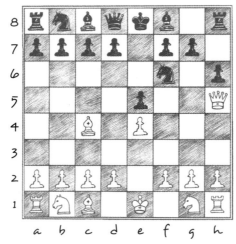

7 | Now you move your Queen from H5 to F7, taking your opponent's Pawn and checkmating your opponent before their jaw can drop.

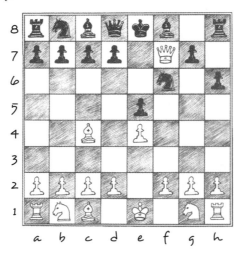

8 | If you want to be particularly mean to conclude your scholar's mate, you can say "Congratulations, you have just been schooled in the game of chess" and shake your bemused opponent's hand.

Learn to deceive

People might tell you that lying is wrong, and they may be right. But we mustn't forget that some professions, such as being a spy or secret agent, require a proficiency in the art of deception. If you are thinking of pursuing such a career, you may want to keep a couple of these points in mind.

What you do

The art of deception requires the following:

1 | Eye contact. You must make eye contact with the person you are deceiving; wandering glances suggest guilt.

2 | A casual action. It is bad to fidget while deceiving, but it is perfectly acceptable to perform a seemingly innocent action, such as polishing your glasses or carefully tying your shoelaces. This will draw people's attention to your action and take attention away from the fact that you are lying.

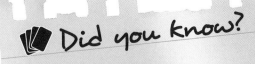

Did you know?

Children learn to deceive convincingly when they are about four years old, and they realize that speaking untruths can save them from punishment for bad behavior.

3 | Natural speech. Try to keep your tone (the level and the rhythm of your speech) consistent with the way you talk when you are honest. High-pitched fast talk will give you away.

4 | Detail. While you shouldn't overexplain anything in a way that suggests guilt, you should feel free to add intricate detail to your deceptions. A lie is more believable if you include details that make people think "Why would she make that up?" For example, "I saw a gorilla on the street" is less believable than "I saw a gorilla on the street and the thing that struck me was its unpleasant and far-reaching smell. I was particularly upset by its sharp, grimy teeth. Did you know that gorillas have incredibly sharp teeth?"

Did you know?

A polygraph, or lie detector, is a device that measures blood pressure, respiration, pulse, and skin conductivity as the subject is asked questions. The polygraph works on the principle that if a person is giving untruthful answers, they will have physical side effects that can be detected by the polygraph.

Keep conversations secret by communicating in codes

Codes are a safe way to send messages without being understood by outsiders. Historically, codes have been used by secret agents and spies, and in wartime.

Scramble code

Scramble code involves changing the order of letters.

What you need

- Paper
- Pen
- An accomplice who knows the code

What you do

1 | Write a message, and then group the letters into fours.
So
MISSION COMPLETED
becomes
MISS IONC OMPL ETED

2 | Then reverse each group.
SSIM CNOI LPMO DETE

3 | Put them together again.
SSIMCNOILPMODETE

4 | You can now pass your message to your accomplice who knows the code (scrambled, groups of four) and who can crack it to reveal your message.

Substituting

Substitution codes work on the principle of swapping letters for other letters or symbols.

Caesar shift

What you need

- Two thin strips of paper

- A pen

Did you know?

This method of coding is called the "Caesar shift," as it was Julius Caesar's preferred way to write secret messages.

What you do

1 | Make some code strips. The lowercase letters represent the "real" alphabet, and the uppercase show your CODE alphabet. Write the "real" alphabet out twice, and the code alphabet once. Side by side the uppercase A is aligned with the first b of the lowercase strip. Like this:

2 | To write your code, all you need to do is line up the code strips as you want them (in this case, a becomes B, but you can slide the strip to have another key, such as a becomes D).

3 | Now you can write your message. So "help me" becomes: GDKO LD. To make it more difficult for people trying to crack your code, you might like to stick the words together, to make GDKOLD. That way, your message will seem like a stream of unintelligible letters, rather than words that can be guessed at.

4 | You and your accomplice both need code strips to be aware of the key letter, in order for this to work.

Deranged alphabet

If you are worried that this substitution code is not secure (a trained spy could probably break it), you can make your code strips a bit trickier. An example is a "deranged alphabet."

What you need

- Two thin strips of paper
- A pen

What you do

1 | Choose a keyword that has no repeated letters. For example, PHOENIX.

2 | Write your "real" alphabet as you did in the Caesar shift.

3 | Then, write out your code strip (UPPERCASE) beginning with your chosen keyword. Then follow with the rest of the alphabet, leaving out the letters in your keyword.

a	P
b	H
c	O
d	E
e	N
f	I
g	X
h	A
i	B
j	C
k	D
l	F
m	G
n	J
o	K
p	L
q	M
r	Q
s	R
t	S
u	T
v	U
w	V
x	W
y	Y
z	Z
a	
b	
c	
d	
e	
f	
g	
h	
i	
j	
k	
l	
m	
n	
o	
p	
q	
r	
s	
t	
u	
v	
w	
x	
y	
z	

4 | Now you can write your coded message following the code strips, as you did for the Caesar shift. This time though, the letters have been mixed up even more.

5 | Your accomplice needs to be aware of your keyword and have their own set of code strips to crack your code.

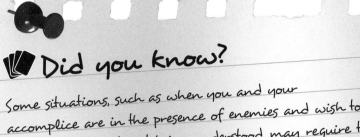

Did you know?

Some situations, such as when you and your accomplice are in the presence of enemies and wish to communicate without being understood, may require the use of scramble talk. Scramble talk can be as simple as reversing words, or whole statements. Those unfamiliar with it will be baffled.

For example: "mission completed" becomes "detelpmoc noissim." It would be pronounced something like "detelp-mock noysim." Once you and your accomplice have practiced a while, you will get the hang of scramble talk, and be able to communicate freely in the presence of spies or enemies.

Hypnotize someone

Before you get excited about mind control, you should understand the principles of hypnosis. Have you ever been in a trance? You have. When you are daydreaming, deeply relaxed or deeply immersed in activity. Hypnosis is when someone else leads you to that state. In this trance state, your unconscious mind is more prone to accept suggestions from your hypnotist by bypassing the conscious mind.

By learning hypnosis you will not be able to create your own army of slaves who will follow your bidding. It is pretty much impossible to hypnotize someone unless they are willing to be hypnotized. Hypnosis is commonly used for various psychological problems such as ego strengthening and pain relief. In a hypnotized state, your mind will be more susceptible to positive suggestions.

What you need

- A willing subject
- A comfortable, quiet environment with a chair
- Dimmed lighting

What you do

This is an example of an induction technique that can be used to put a person into a trance:

1 | Agree with your subject about what you wish to work on during the hypnosis. For example, "We will work on your shyness."

2 | Speak in a calm and moderate voice throughout. Ask your subject to make themselves comfortable in the chair.

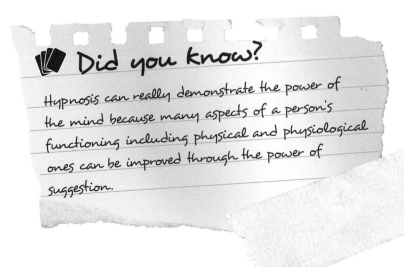

Did you know?

Hypnosis can really demonstrate the power of the mind because many aspects of a person's functioning including physical and physiological ones can be improved through the power of suggestion.

3 | Now it is time to bring them into a meditative, relaxed state. You are going to slow your subject's brain waves to achieve a hypnotic state. Induction techniques vary, but here is one example.

4 | "Now, as you relax, more and more deeply, just allow yourself to float across time and space. Your unconscious mind is going to take you to another place that makes you feel peaceful, calm, safe, and happy. It may be a place you are familiar with, or a place you have never been. Allow yourself to feel calm, relaxed, and happy in this place. You can sit back and rest, or you can walk around, exploring this calm and relaxed place. You might be enjoying touching the things around you, or feeling the cool breeze on your face. The more time you spend in this special place, the more you begin to allow the feelings of peace and calm to flow through you. (Pause.) And as you continue to rest in this place, you will receive the things that you need most. Your unconscious mind knows what you need most. Perhaps you will gain a new perspective, or you will remember an important memory that will help you gain knowledge, or you might hear what you need to hear. Perhaps a soft still voice in your mind will make the suggestions you need now. Even after I've stopped talking you will know that you can return to this special place, whenever you need, to experience the tranquillity of it."

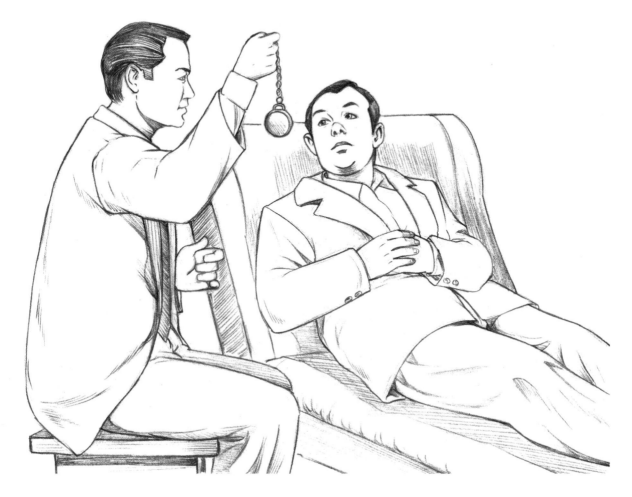

5 | Now that your subject is completely relaxed and in a hypnotic state, you can start making suggestions. For example, if their problem is shyness, you might say, "You are entering a crowded room full of people. All around you are smiling and approving faces and you feel comfortable and relaxed. You enjoy being in the room."

6 | Once you have finished the hypnosis session, gently bring your subject back to reality: "When you are ready to awaken, you can drift back across time and space, bringing the happy and calm feelings and a new sense of perspective with you. And you'll awaken feeling replenished, alert, and calm. What you have experienced can remain with you after you wake up. Now, as I stop speaking, you can continue in this place, receiving what you need, for as long as you like."

Did you know?

People vary in their ability to be hypnotized. Some people are much better hypnotic subjects, which means they can achieve a faster and deeper trance. It means that the phenomenon of hypnotism relies on a person's ability to be hypnotized, not on the hypnotherapist.

SURVIVAL

Tie important knots and stitches

These are all useful. It's a good idea to practice them before you need them.

Round turn and two half hitches

This is an easy knot to fix a rope to something, but it works best when there will always be a pull (some tension) on the main rope.

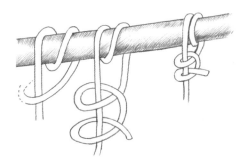

What you do

| 1 | Wrap the rope around twice. |
| 2 | Tie two knots (hitches) in the same direction. |

Reef knot

This fixes the two rope ends – often a rope wrapped round something to hold it together. The rope needs to stay under tension.

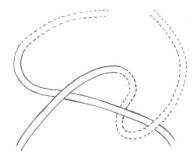

What you do

1	Left over right and under.
2	Right over left and under.
3	You can add a loop (bight) to one end if you want to undo it easily.

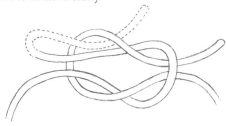

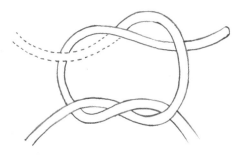

Bowline

This makes a loop that won't slip, but which undoes easily.

What you do

1	Make a loop ("rabbit hole") with the main rope ("tree") on the underside.
2	The end comes up and out through the rabbit hole and around the back of the tree.
3	The end then goes back down the hole.

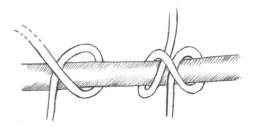

Clove hitch

This can easily be slackened and the rope length changed. It holds when you pull the rope.

What you do

1	Make a round turn and cross over the rope.
2	Take the end round again and push it under the last loop.
3	You can also make it by twisting one loop over another and sliding them both over the end of a post or object.

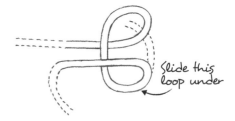

Slide this loop under

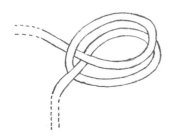

Lashing knot

If you can do this, you will be a true expert! It's used to tie dinghies onto yacht decks, luggage onto roof racks, stop things falling out of trailers and more. It acts like a pulley so that the rope is really tight.

What you do

1	Fix one end to something solid and pass the rope over the load.
2	Loop the free end around something secure.
3	Grab behind the load rope, twist it into a loop, and pull some through to create a slip knot.

4 | Thread the free end through the loop and pull tight. Hold it in place with two half hitches.

5 | If you are feeling really clever, you can add an extra "pulley" slip knot.

6 | To make it easier to undo, you can add a bight loop to the last half hitch.

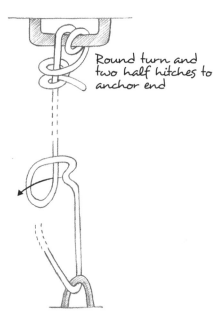

Round turn and two half hitches to anchor end

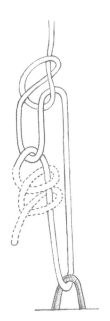

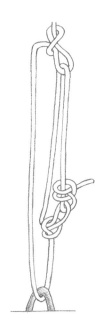

Learn to sew

Knowing how to sew can come in handy in all sorts of situations. Knowing a few basic stitches ahead of time will mean you're already prepared.

Zigzag stitches

Useful for mending tears. Keep them close to start with in an untorn area of fabric, and finish in an untorn area at the other end.

Double sewing

This makes an extra strong seam for joining two layers.

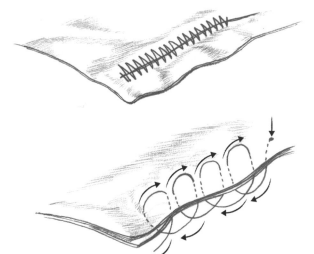

Build a campfire

It's wonderful to sit around a campfire, but such fires have been the cause of many injuries and disasters. Learn how to build a proper campfire.

When choosing your site, make sure that:

- It's at least 3 m (9 ft) from tents, bushes, or other items that can catch fire.

- There are no overhanging branches.

- It's sheltered from winds as much as possible.

- You can put the fire out with water or soil, or you can safely scatter the ashes.

What you need

- Adult supervision.

- Tinder – dry stuff that will burn immediately when lit with a match. Scrunched paper, dead grass, dry leaves, tiny twigs, flakes of bark, wood shavings. Lint from a clothes drier is a favorite, too.

- Kindling – a lot of small dry sticks in a range of sizes from tiny to 2 cm (1 in) in diameter.

- Fuel – larger dry wood that will burn for a long time.

- Matches, gas-powered barbecue lighter, or similar.

- Never start fires with flammable liquids.

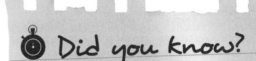

Did you know?

Ashes and burnt logs stay hot for a long time, and many people have been injured, particularly children, by stepping into fires that only appear "dead." Scatter ashes and soak with water until everything is cold before leaving it.

What you do

1. Start with a flat fire-bed in a shallow pit. Place a circle of rocks around it, if you can, and clear about 1 m (3 ft) around the fireplace so the fire won't spread.

2. Have your tinder, kindling, and fuel in separate piles close by.

3. Start with a tennis ball sized loose pile of tinder in the center. Angle small kindling over the top of this in a teepee, volcano, or cone shape, leaving space for air to enter.

4 | With your back to the wind, light the tinder. Fires need air. Gently blow under the tinder if necessary.

5 | As soon as it starts to burn, add more kindling wood, continuing the open cone shape, with air space.

6 | Gradually add larger pieces of wood, always keeping them within the pit or ring. If it starts to go out, add more small kindling.

7 | Make sure it is watched continuously.

Tips

- *Small fires are cozier than enormous ones.*
- *Don't be afraid to cheat and use "fireplace starter" bricks in wet or damp conditions!*

Start a campfire without matches

... or flame-thrower of any kind! Forget about rubbing two sticks together – your chances of lighting a fire this way is just about zero.

The easiest way is to use either a battery or the power of the sun.

What you need

- Adult supervision
- Fresh 9-volt battery
- Pad of fine steel wool (the finer, the better)
- Tinder and kindling wood

What you do

1 | Make sure you have a handful of very fine dry tinder to hand (see previous topic), as well as kindling and fuel wood.

2 | Rub the terminals of the battery on the fine steel wool. The wire will turn red hot and burn.

3 | Quickly add the tinder, gently blow under it if necessary to create flames, and then slope kindling over the top in a cone shape.

Variation

When trying to light tinder using the power of the sun, you can use either something curved and transparent, like a lens, or a curved reflector. If you have a hand lens (magnifying glass), pair of binoculars, or camera lens, they would be ideal.

You can, however, focus the sun's rays onto tinder using a jar or clear plastic bag full of water, or even a shaped block of ice.

Curved reflectors are present in torches and car headlights. Remove the front glass for the best results, and probably the bulb, too.

You can also make one from the curved bottom of a Coke can – but it will need polishing for a very long time until it reflects like a mirror.

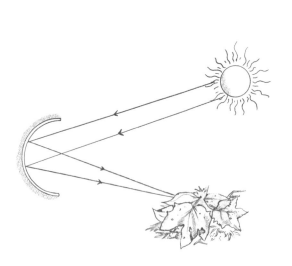

Did you know?

For maximum heat, hold the lens or reflector so that it catches as much sunlight as possible, and move it or the tinder until the smallest (hottest) spot is produced from the sun's rays.

Jump-start a car

If a car's battery is so flat that it will not turn the engine, you can take some power from a car that is working.

What you need

- Purpose-designed jumper leads
- A working car with the same voltage battery
- Safety goggles (preferably)

What you do

If it's possible to call out a mechanic, do so – but if you have to jump-start the car yourself, or tell someone what to do, follow these directions:

1	Check that the battery is not totally flat, cracked, damaged, or frozen (or it could explode). If the car's interior light won't work, the battery's dead – forget about trying to restart the car.
2	Park the cars close enough for the leads to reach from battery to battery, but the cars must NOT touch each other. Open the engine compartment of both cars.
3	Make sure no one is smoking and there are no flames anywhere near – the process produces flammable hydrogen gas.
4	Make sure the hand brakes of both cars are on, their ignition and all electrical things are turned off, and the gears are in neutral or park.
5	Connect the leads in order. One clip of the red + (positive) lead to the + (positive) terminal of the good battery. The positive terminal will probably have several covered wires attached to it. The negative cable is usually single and bare.
6	Connect the other clip of the red lead to the + (positive) terminal of the weak battery.
7	One clip of the black − (negative) lead to the − (negative) terminal of the good battery.
8	Lastly, connect the other clip of the black lead to something hefty, unpainted and metal on the car with the weak battery, for example, the engine block itself. Do NOT attach the clip to the other battery terminal.
9	Stand back and, preferably, wear safety goggles.
10	Start the car with the good battery and let it run for three or four minutes.
11	Start the car with the weak battery and let the engines on both cars run for about five minutes. Both should idle with no hesitation. (If the second car won't start, wait for five minutes and try again. If it still won't start within 30 seconds, give up and call a taxi or a tow truck.)

12 | Before disconnecting the leads, turn on the headlights of the car that had failed. This absorbs some of the power surge that will occur and which can damage the car's computer or fuel injection system. (If you are buying leads, choose a set that is at least 3 m (10 ft) long, heavy gauge, and has "computer protection.")

13 | Disconnect the leads in reverse order.

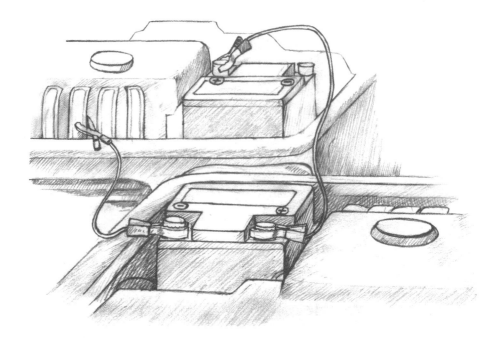

Make a water purifier

Water can contain many things you'd like to remove. Particles of mud and other solids are quite easy to remove, but it's much harder to get rid of toxic chemicals, bacteria, and disease-causing microbes.

Filtering water through layers of gravel will remove particles, and boiling water for 20 minutes will kill disease organisms, but toxins will still remain.

The purest water is produced by distillation – turning water into a vapor and leaving the impurities behind. The pure distilled water condenses into droplets that are collected.

What you need

- Large plastic tub (preferably a dark color)
- Clear plastic sheet (like cling wrap), a bit bigger than the top of the tub
- Sticky tape
- A small pebble or similar
- Cup or jar to collect the pure water

What you do

1 | Put impure water in the bottom of the tub and stand the collecting cup in the center.

2 | Fix the clear plastic sheet to the top of the tub – loose enough so that the center can be weighted down to hang over the cup.

3 | Place the pebble above the cup.

4 | The purified water, which condenses on the plastic sheet, will trickle down to the pebble and drip into the cup.

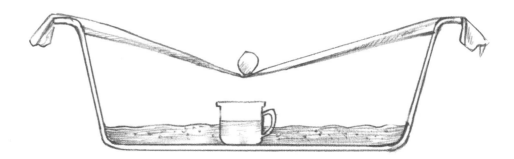

Variation

A larger version can be made outside to collect water from the ground. But the amount of water you catch may be less than the amount of water you lose as sweat in making it – particularly in rocky ground. You need to dig a pit about 0.5 m (1 ft 6 in) deep and 1.33 m (4 ft) across. Use rocks and soil around the edges to anchor a plastic sheet or tarpaulin over the top and, again, place a pebble in the center to make it sag. A cup, container, or cooking pot on the ground, directly under the pebble, will collect water that condenses.

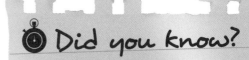

🕐 Did you know?

Car hubcaps make good digging tools. Hikers often take painters' thin plastic drop sheets for emergency use.

Get rescued in the desert

No one should enter a desert alone, and everyone needs to take plenty of water and a survival pack.

Are you really lost, or just "not in the right place"? Don't panic! If you know that you are a relatively short distance to the west of a road that heads north, you may consider walking to the road (but not in the heat of the day, and not when it's dark and you can't see what you're treading on).

Rescuers don't like being hastily called out – but sometimes they are needed. Ideally, you have a navigation device with you to pinpoint your location, and a phone that will tell someone how long you've traveled from your last known starting point. Also report what direction you have been going – you did bring a map and compass, didn't you? – where you think you are, and anyone who's expecting you.

The golden rule for traveling to anywhere remote is (just in case you get out of phone range), before you leave each day, tell someone the name of everyone in your party; when you expect to reach your next destination, or return; your route (and don't deviate from it!); what supplies and equipment you are carrying; your phone numbers; and a rescue service number. Or leave a written note somewhere obvious.

What you do

1. If a car breaks down, stay with it. (The same if you are hiking. Walk a short distance to a hill top or shelter, but don't wander aimlessly, hoping to find something.)

2. Don't eat (it uses water), but drink when you're thirsty – when you run out, your body will be in the best condition to survive.

3. Place rocks, colorful clothing, sheets of newspaper, etc. in the open in the shape of a large X or SOS that can be seen from the air (even if you are with a car). If you are short of things, arrange three items in the shape of a triangle.

4. Light a fire that will make smoke in the day and flames at night. (Burning chunks of spare tire makes lots of smoke.)

5 | If a plane is overhead, you are more likely to be seen if you lie on the ground, cross-shaped, than if you stand and wave.

6 | A mirror can flash light many miles or attract aircraft.

7 | To attract people on foot, whistles carry further than shouts (and don't dry the throat). Whistles or noises (probably not gunshots) in groups of three are recognized as needing help signals.

Warning!

NEVER try out these things just to see if they work. They are for true emergency use only.

Find water in the desert

This is always hard, and walking in the sun and searching may reduce your survival to only a few hours, instead of days. Plants in deserts usually have taproots that go down to water that's a lot deeper than you can dig. And forget trying to get water out of cacti – you'll sweat more than you gain!

What you do

1 | Look out for a flock of birds to see if they land somewhere.

2 | Listen for frogs and try to find them. The place will probably be moist, and there may be water nearby.

3 | Dig a hole in moist soil or sand at the base of a cliff and wait for it to fill (or not).

4 | Dig where different rocks or bands meet and where many plants are growing.

5 | Look for several animal tracks that all lead to the same place.

6 | Clouds of flies may also indicate somewhere moist.

7 | Look for potholes in hard rock in a dried-up riverbed – one may contain water from the last rain.

8 | Dig a hole in the lowest point of a dried-up stream or lake.

9 | Dig in sandy washes on the outside of bends of dried-up streams. If you are lucky, you may find some damp stuff, and can then dig a bigger hole and wait until it fills.

10 | If you find water, stay with it.

Warning!

Be suspicious of water found with no plants growing near to it, or where there are strange mineral deposits. Insect life is a good indicator of water quality. Dead animals are a bad sign.

Tip

Use water-purifying tablets or boil all water for several minutes, if possible.

Avoid getting struck by lightning

Lightning is electricity and likes to find the quickest pathway from clouds to the ground. That means it is attracted to the tallest points and places. It flows easiest through metal things, and easier through water than through wood or air. As your body is mainly water – when you stand upright as the tallest thing in an open place, you become a good target, and an even better target if you hold a spiky umbrella with a metal handle.

What you do

1 | Learn to recognize anvil-shaped storm clouds.

2 | When you see them, remove yourself from a place where you may attract lightning, for example, a mountain top, the ocean (if you're in a boat with a mast), or an open area. Prepare to become safe.

3 | Know that lightning often strikes from the edges of clouds and belts of rain – when you feel the first drops of rain.

4 | Avoid being the tallest thing, or close to the tallest thing around. If you are caught in an open or flat place, keep low, curl yourself into a ball and put your arms over your head and around your ears, and have as little of you as possible touching the ground. (If you are struck, this will minimize damage to your brain, ears, and heart.)

5 | If you can, insulate yourself from the ground by squatting on a pile of climbing rope, or on your backpack (providing it doesn't have a metal frame). Stay there until the storm has passed.

6 | Never shelter under a single tree or isolated patch of trees. The tree might be the initial target, but as you contain more water, the lightning will jump to travel through you, even if you are not touching the tree. It's safer in a wood of even-sized trees than in the middle of a field – but avoid the tallest trees.

7 | Although it's much safer inside a car than being in the open, remove anything made of metal from your body and keep as far from the sides of the car and metal parts as possible.

8 | Avoid the sea's edge – it's often struck, even though nearby cliffs are higher.

9 | Keep away from taps and metal things in a building. Don't use the phone and never take a shower during a storm.

Warning!

Lightning is unpredictable. These tips are not guaranteed. You are never completely safe in a storm.

Build an emergency shelter

The kind of shelter you make will depend on the materials available and the surroundings, but never make one in a streambed, or on the banks – you never know when you may get a flash flood!

What you do

Type 1

If you have large plastic sheet or tarpaulin:

1	Tie a pebble in the center.
2	Hang it from a tree branch.
3	Add rocks around the edges.
4	Or you can fold it over a rope fixed between two trees, and weight the edges.

Type 2

If you have nothing large:

1	Tie a poncho or small plastic sheet between two trees.
2	Fix the bottom edge to the ground with rocks and soil. The aim is for it to slope so that the wind easily blows over the top.
3	If it's likely to rain, fix "drip sticks" to the side ropes so that drips don't run into your dry area.

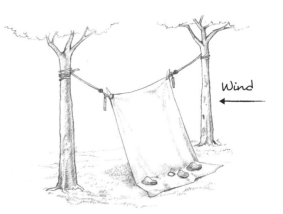

Wind

Type 3

1 | Slope a long central pole (strong branch) from the ground to a fork in a tree, or to a nick in a rock, so that it's secure. Point the end that is on the ground into the wind.

2 | Slope substantial branches and big sticks against the pole, probably on both sides.

3 | Thatch it with leafy branches, with the leaves pointing downward.

4 | Add turf or grass tussocks.

Type 4 – Deep snow

1 | On the sheltered side of a tree, dig a hole against the trunk. With luck, you'll get down to ground level.

2 | Add branches and leaves to sit on.

3 | Add a lid of branches (the best are from fir trees, with leaves on). Make the leaves point downwind.

4 | Snow on the top may provide some insulation.

Type 5 – In the desert

1 | Dig a pit and pile sand into a U shape around it, with the opening downwind. The aim is to encourage the wind to blow over you.

2 | Add and secure whatever you can over the top.

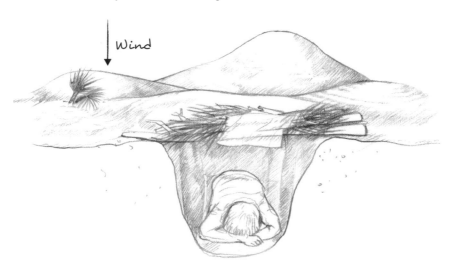

Find south

Some ways to find south depend on whether you are in the southern or northern hemisphere, and some are more accurate than others.

What you do

1 | Look at trees in the open. In the southern hemisphere, over the whole year, the south side of tree trunks get least light. This side will have the heaviest growth of green algae and moss. In the northern hemisphere, the north side of trees is the greenest.

2 | Use a compass. This is more accurate, unless you put your compass close to a wire that is carrying electricity or something made of iron or steel, or you are near the North Pole. Compass needles don't point true north – they point "magnetic north," which is at an angle to true north.

3 | You will be facing south if you stand with your left hand pointing to where the sun rises and your right hand pointing to where it sets.

4 | Outside the tropics, at midday in the southern hemisphere, the sun is due north. It is due south in the northern hemisphere.

Decipher animal tracks

Deciphering animal tracks can make the difference between life and death.

What you do

1 | If you've run out of water, you could follow animal tracks. They may lead you to a supply (but it may not – and you'll have wasted your energy).

2 | Look for signs that animals drink from a water source. If they do drink there, it may be okay for you to do so, too (although it's best to sterilize the water, if possible). If you find dead animals or skeletons nearby – stay thirsty!

3 | Follow tracks backward. Where did they start? The information could lead you to shelter or a source of food.

4 | Look at tracks near water. They could lead you to a safe crossing place, although it's best to be very wary. Large hoof holes in mud hint at what will happen to you if you walk there. Ducks and birds with webbed feet are better equipped to walk on mud than humans, deer, and large mammals, and their prints don't tell you much about mud quality.

5 | The size of crab tracks and excavations can tell you if you are likely to get a reasonable meal after you've dug it out.

Deal with poison bites

Do a recognized Red Cross or St John's Ambulance course to learn how to deal with emergencies and all first aid.

Only people who are very sensitive (have an allergy to the poison) die from insect bites and stings, although swallowing bees and getting stung in the mouth and throat can be dangerous, too. If a rash spreads rapidly over a wide area, a person swells a lot, or becomes short of breath, or their throat feels as though it's closing – immediately phone for an ambulance or quickly get them to a hospital.

What you do

Bees

1	Scrape off the bee's stinger with a credit card or your nail.
2	Don't squeeze the poison sac!
3	Apply an ice pack for pain relief.

Ticks

1	Don't squeeze them or cut them out.
2	Use tweezers underneath them to lever and pull them out – don't cut them out.
3	If one has got you, look everywhere for others that may be hiding.

Wasps, ants, scorpions, and centipedes

| 1 | Pain is helped by ice treatment. That's all most people need. |

Snakes

1	Don't cut, suck, or wash snakebites. Treat them all as possibly deadly and seek help.
2	Put pressure on the site and bandage the spot firmly.
3	Use a second and other bandages over the top to bandage as far up the limb as you can, reasonably tight, but not cutting off all blood flow to fingers and toes (they shouldn't turn color or go cold or numb).

4   Lie the person down, strap their limb to a splint or branch so they can't move their muscles, and immediately call an ambulance.

5   If you are in an isolated place, don't let the person walk unless a car is more than two hours away.

6   Hospitals have antivenom treatments.

7   Try to remember what the snake looked like, or take it with you if it's dead.

Spiders and Scorpions

1   Brown recluse (or violin) and black widow – Wash with soap and water and apply antibiotic lotion. Apply an ice pack wrapped in a cloth. Immediately call an ambulance. For a brown recluse bite, elevate the site to prevent swelling.

2   Scorpions – Wash with soap and water and apply a cold compress. For children, seek medical treatment. Adults will usually not need further treatment.

Fish: stonefish, scorpionfish, stingrays, and others

1   Relieve pain with hot water or ice (but never ice for stingrays).

2   Phone for an ambulance or take to hospital.

3   Do not use pressure.

Cone shell and blue-ringed octopus

1   Apply pressure, as with a snake bite.

2   Send for an ambulance.

Bluebottle jellyfish (Portuguese man-of-war) and corals

1   Only wash with sea water – not vinegar.

2   Apply dry cold packs.

3   Get help, especially if stung over a large area.

Box jellyfish

1 | Wash the stung area with vinegar.

2 | Use pressure bandaging, as for a snake bite.

3 | Call an ambulance.

Dogs

1 | Use antiseptics against bacteria and viruses.

2 | Dogs in some countries carry rabies, from which you can die.

3 | Get immediate medical help.

Ace a spelling test

People usually learn things from a mixture of looking, listening, and doing – but mostly, everyone prefers one of these styles more than the others for easy learning. Do you know how you learn best? If you were reporting a race, would you first talk about the colors of the cars and the flash as they go by, the howling noise they make, or the spinning of wheels and swerving around corners?

"Visual" people will look longest at a list of words to remember them.

"Listening" people will say them out loud many times, letter by letter.

"Doing" people might play tennis and call out the letters in time with hitting the ball, or call them out while skipping or running, or just write them many times.

What you do

1 | Use a mixture of all these methods.

2 | Split words into small chunks so they are less com-plic-ated.

3 | Make up memory aids – mnemonics (pronounced "nih-MON-icks"). For example, how do you remember if greetings cards are a kind of "stationery" or "stationary"? Answer: envelope starts with E – so the correct spelling is stationery.

4 | If you find particular words difficult, write each one many times on scraps of paper and put them all round the house in places where you stop and where you will see them, for example, by the phone, in the bathroom, on the dining table, and by the clock.

5 | Make a list of words to remember on a pocket-sized card. Look at it often when you are waiting for the bus to arrive or for other things to happen.

Get the better of a bully

Bullies will always exist in schools, in neighborhoods, and even in factories and workplaces. Maybe even in retirement homes. They want to get you to do something – like, freak out. Just because they do bad things, it isn't smart to do bad things to get back at them.

What you do

1 | Stay calm and act normal. Try and hide your knocking knees. If the bully can't get a reaction from you, you become no fun to hassle.

2 | Tell them to knock it off. If a bully is not told to stop, they will keep doing the same thing. Some children are used to, and enjoy, "rough play" at home and don't realize that "quiet" people find their style annoying. Say "Stop!" and calmly walk away.

3 | If a bully tries to make fun of you, try to make an even funnier joke about yourself. Many professional comics learned their skills this way. If you are a fun person, the bully would rather hear your jokes than hurt your feelings.

4 | Talk to your friends about the bully and what is happening.

5 | If there is a bully about, try to stay close to other people. Never be alone.

6 | If the bully still keeps bothering you, let an adult know. A teacher, parent, counselor, or boss may be able to help. You can work together to make the situation better.

7 | At a time when a bully is making your life difficult, think about your friends. They are the ones that are important to you.

Make friends when you're new

When you know no one in your new school, town, or job, life may feel less fun. But now you have a chance to be the sort of person you really want to be – including being the most popular person in the place.

What you do

1 | Walk tall and with confidence, with your head up. Pretend that you have been around for ages, even if you feel nervous. If you appear in control and cool, people will believe that you are.

2 | As you pass people, look them in the eye and smile.

3 | If a person smiles back at you, or nods their head, tell them your name and find out what theirs is. Use it next time you meet.

4 | Compliment people. Tell them you like something they are wearing. You'll soon be in conversation. Ask questions. Tell them you are thinking of buying a car like theirs – ask what it's like. People like talking about themselves and they like people who are interested in them.

5 | Introduce yourself to people around you. "Hi, my name's _____. I don't think we've met before. And you are…?" Keep using the names of people you talk to. It will help you to remember them. Don't be afraid to say, "I have met so many new people, I'm afraid I have forgotten your name. What was it again?" People understand and like the fact that you really want to get to know them. Make a big effort to learn a few more names every day.

6 | Find out what people like to do and see if you have the same interests. Try to talk to them about something that is important to them.

7 | Advertise what interests you. Have your favorite book open. You may attract someone who likes the same thing.

8   Ask for help. "I missed last night's episode of _____. Can anyone tell me what happened, please?" You've just found someone with a similar interest and who's friendly and helpful! Most people like to be friendly and help others.

9   Help others when you can, too.

Defend yourself

Unfortunately, people exist who may wish to attack you or steal. Ideally, you should take a proper self-defense course – but read a kung fu manual, at least, to learn some moves and practice them.

What you do

1   Always be aware of what is happening around you and look alert.

2   Avoid showing that you have things of high value.

3   Do not look nervous or lost – even if you are.

4   Avoid being alone. Keep where there are other people about.

5   If you feel in danger, turn and run away.

6	If you are attacked, scream.
7	Kick, scratch, bite, stamp, elbow – do what is necessary. (You can easily injure yourself by punching.)
8	Know that good weapons are hands, fingers, knees, elbows, heels, shoes, keys, combs, and phones. Use the side of your hand to chop, or the "heel" of your hand (the end of the arm bone) like giving a high five.

Targets

- Eyes – Poke, gouge, or spit in them.

- Nose – Hit it with the heel of your hand, elbow, or knee for pain and to knock off balance. Pull nostrils.

- Ears – Pull, twist, or bite them. You can use them to move the head to where you can hit another part. A hard hand slap can also deafen.

- Chin – An upward hit is good to unbalance the person. It could also make them bite their tongue. Use your knee, head, elbow, or palm.

- Neck and throat – Dig fingers in around the bottom of the windpipe, where it meets the collarbone. Strangling, hitting, or gouging the windpipe can also be effective.

- Body – Being hit in the solar plexus (at the front, just below the ribs) makes people double up. The tummy is a good target, too.

- Hands – Stamp on them with pointed heels.

- Groin – Nothing hurts a man more than a kick or knee in the testicles. Grab them if you have to.

- Knees – Stamp on them or kick them from in front to bend them the wrong way, or stamp from behind to unbalance.

- Shins – Kick them or scrape them with your shoe.

- Ankles – People will find it harder to run after you if you stamp on their ankles, knees, or feet with pointed heels or the back edge of flat ones.

- Feet – Aim for the top of the foot or the toes, especially if wearing stilettos.

Learn Morse code

Morse code was developed by Samuel F.B. Morse in the 1840s (before telephones were invented) to send messages along telegraph wires as electrical pulses. At the other end, they could be "printed" as dents in a paper tape.

Morse code is still useful. All letters, numbers, and signs (like, "this is the end of the message") can be made from short and long sounds, flashes, pulses, or marks. Quick ones are "dots" or "dits," and long ones "dashes" or "dahs."

What you do

For survival, spell out SOS, which stands for Save Our Souls – help is needed. In Morse code this is:

dot dot dot	dash dash dash	dot dot dot
• • •	— — —	• • •
S	O	S

Remember, this can be signaled using a torch or by uncovering a light. Or, if you are buried or locked in, you can tap it on metal pipes, for example, or bang it on the wall (and people will know that you are not just doing repairs). You can whistle it, if you are out in a wild place. Or sound your car or boat horn.

Tips

If a dot/dit is one unit long, a dash/dah is three units long, the gap between letters is three units, and, if you ever use the code for words, put seven units of space or quiet between them. If a letter is made of dots and dashes, separate them with a one unit space.

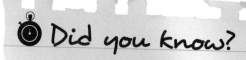

Did you know?

People who learn the whole alphabet can send messages quicker than texting with their phone.

Warning!

Only ever use SOS in a true emergency. Never try it out just to see if people really will come.

The Morse alphabet

A	· —	N	— ·	O	— — — — —
B	— · · ·	O	— — —	1	· — — — —
C	— · — ·	P	· — — ·	2	· · — — —
D	— · ·	Q	— — · —	3	· · · — —
E	·	R	· — ·	4	· · · · —
F	· · — ·	S	· · ·	5	· · · · ·
G	— — ·	T	—	6	— · · · ·
H	· · · ·	U	· · —	7	— — · · ·
I	· ·	V	· · · —	8	— — — · ·
J	· — — —	W	· — —	9	— — — — ·
K	— · —	X	— · · —	Fullstop	· — · — · —
L	· — · ·	Y	— · — —	Comma	— — · · — —
M	— —	Z	— — · ·	Query	· · — — · ·

Escape from being tied up

We've all seen our favorite action star escape from being tied up by the bad guy. So how does he do it? You will need all your strength, and it will help if you are flexible and can twist your body around.

What you do

1 | Make your body as big as possible while you are being tied. Fill your chest with air, try to hold your ankles and wrists as far apart as you can, and clench your fists and arch your feet to expand your muscles. If you are being tied in a chair, push on the ground with your feet so that your bottom is loose on the seat.

2	If your mouth has been sealed with tape, keep licking it round the edges and rub it on something to get it off. Try chewing it.
3	If tape is round other parts of your body, try to chew it off or get it off with your mouth. Or you may be able to reach with fingernails.
4	Look for things you can rub tape or rope against, to cut it or wear it away. It's easier to wear through tape.
5	Try to get your hands free to loosen other knots.
6	Use your strength and muscles to straighten or bend your body to stretch rope – then relax and see if you have more room to wriggle out.
7	Use the fingers on your strongest hand to push the other hand out of the knot.

Learn basic first aid

Everyone should do a course run by the Red Cross, St John's Ambulance, or similar organization to learn the correct methods for dealing with emergencies, bandaging, and more. A first aid handbook is excellent – make sure it's the latest one.

What you do

- Choking – If the person can still talk, don't slap their back, just encourage them to keep coughing, face down, with their head lower than their chest.

- Swallowed poison – Don't give food or liquid until you have checked with a professional. Immediately phone the Poison Control Center (in the USA) or a hospital and tell them, if you can, what the person has taken. In the USA, the number is 1-800-222-1222. Keep a vomit sample for testing. They will probably need to go to hospital.

- Minor burns – Do not apply ice, ice-cold water, oil or cream, or burst blisters. Put under cool running water for 20 minutes, or keep applying cool wet cloths (to the face, for example). Remove rings – a finger will swell. Cover with sterile gauze or cloth. Most burns heal quickest and with minimal scarring if kept moist with medical burn gel. Get medical help.

- Sprained ankles and knees – Apply an ice pack (ice sealed in a plastic bag – but always wrap the bag in a damp cloth) over the whole area – 10 minutes on, 10 minutes off for up to 72 hours, and raise up the limb. After 72 hours of cold, a doctor may recommend heat.

- Minor cuts – Use antiseptics, not disinfectant. Use scrubbed hands and sterile swabs to remove anything that has caused the cut and to clean it. A sterile gauze pad and a bandage applying some pressure should stop bleeding. Don't bandage so tight that the limb, toes, or fingers turn color and go numb. Seek help if the bleeding doesn't soon stop.

When unsure, see a doctor immediately or phone for an ambulance.

Change a tire

Changing a tire yourself should not take long or require great strength – but you will get dirty! Note: keep gloves in with the spare.

What you do

1 | Put hazard lights on.

2 | Get the car out of the way of passing traffic and on to somewhere hard and flat.

3 | Put the hand brake on, turn off the engine, and put the car in gear or in "park."

4 | Slow other motorists with something (preferably a safety triangle), or somebody waving up and down, at least 10 meters (10 yards) down the road.

5 | Take out the spare and lay it flat.

6 | Put a chock (brick, chunk of wood, or rock) under at least one wheel on the opposite side of the car to the flat tire.

7 | Put the jack on hard flat ground under a place on the car recommended by the maker. Raise the car just a little.

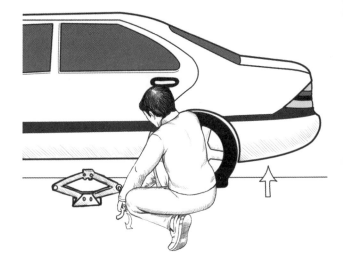

8 | Lever off the hubcap.

9 | With straight arms and back, use the brace (big spanner) to fractionally loosen all nuts by turning them anticlockwise. You can stand on the brace if necessary.

10 | Jack up the car much higher so that there's enough room for the new tire to fit.

11 | Remove all the wheel nuts and keep them very safe.

12 | Remove the wheel and lay it flat.

13 | Line up the holes in the spare with the studs (screw threads), and then lift it into position.

14 | Screw the nuts on finger tight (try the bottom one first; then the wheel will stay there), and then give them a small "nip" with the brace – not hard, or the car could fall off the jack.

15 | Let the car down completely and remove the jack.

16 | Use the brace to do the nuts up in opposite pairs, all averagely tight to start with, and then with an extra pull to get them really tight. Only use your arms (remember – straight back!) – no feet or jumping on it. Have the handle horizontal for the final pull on each one.

17 | Put back the hubcap (though it's not essential), take the chocks away, and make sure you take everything with you – flat tire, brace, jack, safety triangle …

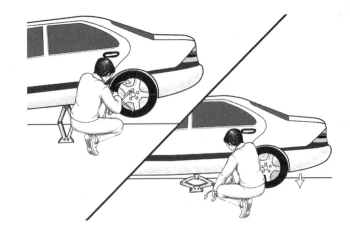

Save money

Fact: If you don't have money in your pocket or wallet, you won't spend it. Just carry enough for an emergency phone call and a bus home. There are plenty of other ways to save money.

What you do

1 | Make a list of things you need and must buy when you go out – not things you want. Can you make do without something? Only buy what's on the list. Buy as little as you can.

2 | Don't go near shops unless you have to.

3 | Save loose change in a jar. It will soon add up.

4 | Buy all presents at sales, or make them yourself. People treasure gifts you have made especially for them.

5 | Pass on books and toys to other people or do a swap.

6 | Car pool.

7 | Discover what skills your neighbors have and what they need, and barter – swap a haircut for mowing a lawn or paint their fence in exchange for something they can do for you.

8   Buy things from charity stores and sales, or through private advertisements in the local newspaper – but not just because they are cheap. Nothing is a bargain if you don't need it.

9   Many broken things can be mended more cheaply than buying replacements.

10   Grow fruit and vegetables. Swap the surplus with other people.

11   Turn off all lights and electrical equipment (at the wall) when they're not in use.

12   Don't buy pets. Offer to look after those belonging to neighbors – they may even pay you. They may also pay you to water their plants when they go on holiday.